A New New Me

by the same author

PEACES
PARASOL AGAINST THE AXE

A NEW NEW ME

HELEN OYEYEMI

faber

First published in 2025
by Faber & Faber Limited
The Bindery, 51 Hatton Garden
London EC1N 8HN

Typeset by Faber & Faber Limited
Printed and bound by CPI Group (UK) Ltd, Croydon, CR0 4YY

A CIP record for this book
is available from the British Library

ISBN 978–0–571–38752–6

Printed and bound in the UK on FSC® certified paper in line with our continuing
commitment to ethical business practices, sustainability and the environment.
For further information see faber.co.uk/environmental-policy

Our authorised representative in the EU for product safety is
Easy Access System Europe, Mustamäe tee 50, 10621 Tallinn, Estonia
gpsr.requests@easproject.com

2 4 6 8 10 9 7 5 3 1

A New New Me

MONDAY

Hi girls,

Kinga-Alojzia here. It's almost bedtime, and I'm at the kitchen table beginning our diary for the week of 26 February 2024.

This is a voice transcription. It had to be. I've got lots to tell you; it'd take ages to write it down. I'm whispering as a precaution against being overheard, so I'm not sure how this will turn out. I'll check the punctuation before I close my eyes. For now I'm watching these words rushing along the screen, crashing into each other, splitting, trembling for the blink of an eye as letters are substituted. Vowels spin like roulette wheels while the program waits for me to finish pronouncing a word. It's you I'm talking to, not my phone . . . still, it's hard to imagine a keener listener than AI.

An example: just today I exchanged personalised news alerts with Eva from work. We began doing that with the expectation that sooner or later the information that's been gathered about our browsing habits will lead us to the same corners of the internet. That's what's supposed to happen when an algorithm scans the online behaviour of two women in their early forties who send each other copious amounts of memes, sign the same petitions, have the same reproduced map of Narnia hung up on the wall behind their desks and pounce on the same bargains at the same times: Christmas decorations on

26 December, yes. Real chocolate – that is, the French, Swiss or Belgian stuff – the day after St Valentine's, yes. Black Friday, no. But we've been comparing notes for seven years, and our news alerts are yet to meet in the middle.

'So, what's today's top bulletin?' Eva asked me.

'Oh . . . these are such troubling times, Eva. The Luxury Enamel Posse has struck again.'

'What? The what?'

'The Luxury Enamel Posse,' I said, enunciating as clearly as I could. 'No, I understood that part,' Eva said. 'You speak such nice Czech, Kinga—' (sorry, girls, I couldn't resist taking this moment to imitate Eva in Condescending Mode. It's possibly her cutest mode. I genuinely mean that, but also patronising one's patroniser is a victory of sorts, so just let me have it). 'You speak such nice Czech, Kinga, but what is this Posse?'

'Oh, you never heard about them? They invade your home just before dawn, fold you up into a suitcase and fill the remaining suitcase space with loose teeth and blank cheques. Then they zip up the case and leave.'

Eva began stapling forms, BAM, BAM, BAM. 'Ježíš Maria,' she said. 'As if we don't have enough on our plates.'

I raised my phone so she could see I was referring to a reputable news source. 'So, ah, as it says here, this time the LEP visited a family of three in Chodov. Mother, father, ten-year-old son, all three toothed up and chequed out. The kid's suitcase was left partially unzipped, so he managed to get out and unpack his parents, but I think gymnastics classes are the real hero here, because when you look at how they had his arms around his ankles—'

'Is that their main stomping ground, then? Chodov?' Eva was getting her hopes up, looking for ways to make this one neighbourhood's concern. She lives in Střešovice, so all she knows is the soft life. Because what's Střešovice, really . . . if you ask me, that place isn't much more than a garden with houses sprinkled on top.

'No,' I told her. 'So far they've popped up all over Prague. I suppose if they stuck to one postal code they'd have been caught long ago.'

That elicited another *Ježíš Maria* from my work wife, and a question: 'When we say "crew", are we talking about five or six people?'

'More like thirteen or fourteen, or so their victims say. Some of them do the tooth- and cheque-stuffing, while others, ah, stand around pointing and laughing, or eating snacks they've actually brought with them. In a couple of instances, neighbours who thought they were hearing a house party have knocked on the front door to have a grumble, and the Crew immediately dropped everything and swooped out onto the street,' I consulted my phone, 'like a flock of bats.'

'So now I've got to lie in bed trying to decide whether the racket from the floor above is just some selfishness I can sleep through, or I'm listening to this Luxury Crew's latest target and only my hostility can shorten the ordeal? It's too exasperating. What exactly is their objective?'

'That's what we'd all love to know, Eva. But no one even

has a clue where to begin speculating.'

'Alright, setting aside the cheques, what about all those loose teeth? Who do they belong to?'

'That's still under investigation.'

'They must have had at least a few of those teeth analysed at a lab by now,' Eva said, pointing her stapler at me and narrowing her eyes.

'Apparently the teeth don't match dental records held anywhere in the country. Look, I'm not happy about it either, but what can we do? Now: what did *your* phone urgently want to tell you today?'

'Oh, it's wonderful news,' Eva said, showing me a somewhat blurred photo. Its subject, a lean and brindled rabbit, appeared to be snarling slightly. Three gold medals lay at the rabbit's feet. You could sense that this had been a tricky photoshoot. This was a portrait of a winner who'd guarded her medals, refusing to be decorated with them and making it clear that a close-up shot was out of the question. 'Marketa's the only bunny in the entire history of the European Rabbit-Hop Championships to take first place in three different events. She got gold medals for the flat track, park run *and* long jump events. And the best part is, she's Czech. A hardworking resident of Ústí nad Labem who trained every day, rain or shine.'

An inspiration to us all. Franta, Valérie, Pavlína and I took a five-minute break and gathered round Eva's computer to watch Marketa of the former Sudetenland conquering every obstacle set in her path. The Rabbit-Hop Champion left me no room for my usual scepticism as to whether I'm dealing with a person who's really trying their best. This Marketa was a compact unit of concentration, pounding away at the air like a fist. She was news I wouldn't have had the faintest inkling of if not for Eva.

Speaking of ultimate effort, girls . . . I've unregistered our Wolt account again. This time I'm begging you not to reinstall the app for at least another three months. You've already placed enough food-delivery orders for a lifetime. I've looked over the receipts, I've looked at menu photos, and you ladies can't be serious. You're joking with me, and I can't laugh – I'd need to find the stamina first. We're a forty-year-old with places to go and things to do. You can't really think that pale amber-tinted broths and avocados sliced in half and covered with wildflowers are the winning formula that meets our daily needs. It's just not possible for any of the Kingas our grand-mother raised to be this out of touch. Not only would Babcia have gone off on one if she'd ever found out about all of this, but she'd have been justified for once. What happened to the frugal ways we were taught? And do you not see that at this rate our arms are liable to dwindle to toothpicks? That's not a physique we can afford; nobody can. Anyone who intends to keep living in this complicated world has to be able to wield a rolling pin (or similar) in the unhinged manner Babcia did that night Dad crashed through the bathroom window roaring that nobody ever spares a thought for a father's love and she'd almost made up her mind to let him say his piece until she saw he hadn't even had the common courtesy to take his shoes off in her home. I know it was Dziadek's home, too, but they took

7

care of the place in different ways. Dziadek's ways were all the level-headed ones that involved an infinitely expanding box of spanners, screwdrivers and all sorts of other bits he referred to as 'thingies'. *Pass the thingy . . .* Nobody likes their placidity being taken for granted; I saw him try to show us some anger from time to time. He never even made it to indignation – it was like he couldn't find his way there, and, discovering that he was too proud to ask for directions, he turned around and went home to his main facial expression, the one that was half indifference and half polished cordiality. If Dziadek had ever laid down his book of the day and watched TV he'd have known what I meant when I once told him he'd make a perfect game show host. But he didn't, so he didn't.

Emboldened by the feeling that he wouldn't mind, I've tried to saddle him with the blame for our pie-in-the-sky tendencies – *Oh, that's who we take after, it's Dziadek* – but really it must've been the novels themselves that did it. We'd never have ended up needing what we now think of as 'more' if not for all those eats characters keep enjoying in books. Do crumpets actually taste of anything, or have we been brainwashed? It's probably too late to answer that.

I get it, that's all I'm trying to say. I get it, I accept that our tastes have been formed, and I'm not interested in making anyone feel guilty about what makes them happy. I could always feel the Lenten fast trying to do those things to us when we were younger, so this request is nothing like that. No deprivation! Just . . . let's prepare the character-in-a-novel feasts at home, please. We've got all the ingredients. Check the freezer: I tracked down unagi fillets. In the cupboard directly above the washing machine you'll find a vial of balsamic vinegar that's been aged for fifty years. We've got burrata, pink tomatoes, sufficient nourishment and sufficient variety. Just think . . . if you co-operate, we'll be able to walk faster. I have no doubt that if Kinga-E makes any response to this at all, it'll be something along the lines of 'There are no benefits to rushing . . .' Which, with all due respect, is more or less what you'd expect from someone who spends most of their time either at the cinema or submerged in shrubbery. The rest of you might find it worthwhile to ask yourselves why we should keep being late for work, appointments, social engagements, everything, when an easy adjustment to energy intake would make us perfectly capable of catching buses on time?

Enough nagging. I've just remembered some other good news: we're Czech passport holders now! I was up early to collect our passport from the Municipal Office this morning. Apart from that highlight, Monday was its usual self, up to a point. I was up at six, got the washing and brushing out of the way, crunching on instant coffee granules and repeating Snoop Dogg's daily affirmations as I applied rouge until there was enough of it to make any other make-up unnecessary. It had all paid off, all the studying, the form-filling, the queuing, the practice tests, the proofs of income, the presentation of documents for notarisation, the swearing of an oath of loyalty and obedience. A personal rabbit race of sorts. 'Být mnou je to nejlepší, co se člověku může přihodit,' I said, bobbing my head to the beat and turning the volume up so that the California velvet of Snoop's voice rolled out over mine. I could copy him exactly, but it's Czech I need to keep practising, not English . . . 'Dnes bude úžasný den!' Then, tapping my own chest, with deep conviction, 'Moje pocity jsou DŮLEŽITÉ.' *There's no one better to be than myself. Today is going to be an amazing day! My feelings MATTER.*

After all the affirmations had been made, I set the timer for twenty minutes and played the dressing-up game, putting outfits on and taking them off until the alarm made the final decision. And I was half an hour early for my passport-collection appointment. I took a ticket number and a seat in a waiting room with the kind of strip lighting that makes you feel like orange juice has been splashed on your eyeballs every time you look up. When I sat down, every fragment of plastic in my chair that had even the slightest squeak in it squeaked with all its might, but the only person that looked around was a cheerful-looking seventy-something brunette in a dark-turquoise cape and matching ankle boots. I gave her a careful once-over, as her cheerfulness did not seem harmless. You know when you meet someone who's in possession of information that's great for them but tough luck for you? That's what this woman's cheerfulness was like. Imbued with venom that tenses all your muscles and improves your hearing and eye-sight. Another thing: this sounds silly, because looks-wise she blended in well enough (she could very easily have been there renewing her passport rather than picking up a brand-new one) but I could tell that this lady was there for the same reason as I was. She continued to stare – I looked away, looked back at her and she was still staring. I brushed my hand across my lips really quickly, hoping to dislodge any instant coffee granules that might have made me an oddity. She went on staring until I said: 'Er . . . good morning?'

She replied with a whispered accusation: 'You're *famous*.'

'No, I'm not,' I whispered back, 'By the way – isn't this the first time we've met?' (She'd addressed me as *jsi* instead of using the more formal *jste*; her language teacher must've been lax with instructions on how to speak to strangers.)

'You are famous,' she said, sticking with *jsi*. 'You're . . . oh, you know – the lion-tamer. Not at all concerned about losing any fans, I see – scrabbling around in your bag like that when your public is trying to talk to you . . .'

My eyes began to cross slightly; I was watching her *and* the clock on the wall. What if this was the Final Boss stage of the citizenship test? Doom felt close by. At the very last minute, the passport held beneath my nose would be whisked away, either because this woman had distracted me and made me late, or because I'd forgotten one or all of the documents I'd been told I had to bring. I double checked. My ID card was there, my certificate of citizenship was there, the appointment letter was there. I relaxed enough to tell her that she'd mistaken me for someone else.

The woman arranged her fingers into a rectangle and held them up in front of my face and looked at me through the rectangle, her eyes glinting like dark sequins. 'Are you saying you're not . . . ?'

'No, I'm not him.'

'You know who I mean, though?'

'There's only one person you could be thinking of, ma'am.'

'Who?' she asked, lowering her hands.

There were still twenty minutes left to wait. OK, I thought. I've met this lady at an auspicious time; here we both are, having our fresh start. We can congratulate each other, we can talk. I told her my name, and she told me hers. A nice name: Milica. I asked her what had brought her to Prague, since people seem to like being asked such things. She was an exception to this rule. Frowning, she answered that, having worked out that she'd been conceived here, she'd come back to show the city what it had done. I think I mumbled something like 'Oh . . . OK . . .'

'Now then,' she said, her gaze flicking between me, the clock and the screen that showed the ticket numbers of those whose time had come, 'unless you have any other generic questions for me, how about telling me who I thought you were?'

'Oh . . . you thought I'm my brother. You must've just seen the movie he's in; he had to grow his hair long for that. *A Tale Told by No One to No One*.'

'Yes, that's it.' Milica nodded with an expression that made it hard to tell how she felt about the film. We traded a few (probably misremembered) quotes and impressions, an exchange that covered a number of different modalities. We could've been two admirers of the film emphasising what struck them, two unimpressed viewers broadcasting scorn, or a fangirl fangirling while a mocker mocks. When you're just quoting like that, there's no pressure to reveal what side you're on. The unloveliest girl in the sultan's harem clings to surviv-al by finding ways to surprise her lord and make him laugh; she becomes the sultan's pet, not seen or treated as a concu-bine, but favoured above all the greatest beauties of her age. Meanwhile, the son of a disgraced janissary curls up to sleep with the sultan's lions night after night; the lion cages are the only corners of the kingdom nobody dares follow him into. We can only guess what the lions make of all this: perhaps, noticing how hard the humans beat this boy, the lions com-pare that mercilessness to the way they're whipped by their attendants. From the lions' point of view, the humans could be ganging up on the boy because they fear him. And what could be more fearsome to humans than a lion? His phys-ique is admittedly ridiculous, but this trembling two-legged being must be a lion by nature, a lion just like them, having to take blows from lesser creatures with the pathetic need to feel more powerful than they really are. Having made sense of the boy's presence amongst them, the lions cleave to him – he is their boy, he's permitted to play with their cubs, they join in the fun too, in their own way, by copying things he does. In his manhood – here's where my brother takes over from the adolescent actor – the adopted lion comes to the sultan's attention, and, led by his gestures, all the other lions stand to attention in the sultan's presence. This is a big hit with every-body, and a display that scares Christian visitors out of their wits. Until, one night, fleeing from yet another messenger sent by the sultan's consort, the lion-tamer runs into a strange woman who tells him she's been thinking it'd be fun to get eaten by lions and has to be restrained from rushing into the cage he was about to enter himself. Of course, from then on, these two malcontents make us ringside spectators to a crazy and catastrophic love affair that's even crazier and even more catastrophic than we were prepared for. The kind that ends with nobody left to tell the tale of all he did for her sake, and she for his.

'Aren't those two together in real life?' Milica asked.

'Nah.'

'Are you sure? I mean, there's convincing and *convincing* . . .'

These were insinuations I used to make. Then Benek invited me on set. It's hard to tell if that was a deliberate move to nip those comments in the bud; I've heard him try to reframe them as testaments to his and Thuso's level of craft. Either way, I'm not Benek, so . . . 'That's called acting,' I explained. 'And it was one facet of a cosmos of considered decisions made by a huge team of professionals who were wholly committed to showing you a Fool and a lion-tamer in love. Please don't devalue all the labour that made it possible to feel convinced by what you saw.'

'Prickle, prickle! Alright . . . I'm finally starting to feel like he might actually be your brother after all.'

'What? Why would I lie about that?'

'It's unclear,' she said. 'It's just . . . why haven't you said his name? You could easily have finished my sentence when I asked about it.'

'Oh,' I said. 'I don't finish people's sentences for them.'

We swapped shiny smiles, I checked the items in my bag

14

again, then Milica sighed, pulled out her phone and looked up the movie she'd told me I'd appeared in.

'Benedykt Sikora,' she read aloud.

'Yes. That's my brother.'

'It must be a pain, looking so similar people get you mixed up.'

'Most people don't. And a few do it on purpose.'

'Pfffft. No need to be like that about it. You looked very familiar, that was all I knew. So. What's he really like, then?'

Benek. My Benek. Suddenly I wanted to tell this stranger about how when my movie-star brother was little, about four or five, he used to stagger over to wherever I was with his nose running, blow that slimy nose of his on my t-shirt and then stagger off with his arms raised, yelling 'KINGA IS A HANKY! THE BEST HANKY!' That disgusting brat grew up into an almost comically considerate sibling, husband and father who says that hanky story simply can't be true, he was always in far too much awe of his big sister to ever treat her like that. I wanted to tell Milica that we debated this and a lot of other things when we quarantined together at his seaside shack in Finisterre – just the two of us, my brother and me. That was in 2020, but it feels like it was just last month. Benek was too sick to talk as much as he did – and so was I. But there was something like a tide of speech coursing between our rooms, murmurs of grief got in under the doors and laughter rattled off the ceilings. We heard each other everywhere, and couldn't bear to turn off the sound.

'Benek is OK,' I said. 'I like him.'

Milica's ticket number came up, and she told me she'd wait for me outside. 'Oh,' I said. 'I didn't realise there was anything left to say . . . ?'

'I lost a friend a while ago, and it's high time I made a new one,' she said, squeezing my shoulder as she stood up. 'I won't beat around the bush, Kinga: you meet my requirements. I'm sure I can meet yours too! Let's talk once we've got what we came for.'

With those words she turned the collection of my passport from an event I'd been looking forward to for weeks to minutes of polite toe-tapping while I wondered what it was that Milica had in mind. She was waiting on the street outside and greeted me with a frolicsome foot-shuffle and a faceful of tobacco smoke. We briefly swapped compliments on the photo pages of our brand-new IDs, then found ourselves seats at the nearest cafe, where she asked me about my requirements for friendship.

'Well . . . one requirement is . . . disclosure of *your* requirements,' I told her. 'How could you possibly know whether I meet them?'

'A word of advice, Kinga,' she said, reaching into the bowl of sweeteners set on the table between us. She separated the packets of sugar from the packets of stevia and pocketed the stevia. 'Don't ask anybody why they like you. It's exactly the same as begging to be mistreated. So . . . simply be assured that you'll do. Now, back to what you appreciate in a person!'

A minute of silence passed, then two. Milica seemed to like it; she seemed happy to leave this silence unbroken for all eternity unless I took my own turn to speak. 'What do I appreciate . . . um. A good sense of boundaries is important,' I muttered.

'Could you be a bit more specific?'

'Yes. You shouldn't ask too many questions,' I said. 'And you can only contact me on Mondays.'

'OK.'

We made a clinking gesture with our coffee cups.

'What else?' she asked.

'Well, you said you'd lost a friend and need a new one. I'd like to know more about that.'

'Alright,' Milica said, 'but I have a question first. Hope I'm allowed to at least ask this one.'

'Go on . . .'

'What do you do?'

'For work? I'm a matchmaker.'

'Matchmaking as in, bringing couples together for romance?'

'Well, partnership is the main objective. Whilst not exactly discouraged, romance is far from compulsory.'

'Huh. Freelance?'

'No, corporate actually.'

Milica's eyebrows flew up like kites as I explained about having started out as a teller at a Łódź branch of a well-known bank, then transferring to the bank's Prague headquarters to take a job that had been created in response to the Fidelity Awards the Senate started handing out last year. The award ceremonies are televised: couples who've been together for fifty years or more get to shake hands with the President and her husband. Then the half-century couple is presented with certificates and made the subject of laudatory speeches. The couple's children and grandchildren are interviewed, we hear from every beneficiary of the stability these couples have provided. It's a buffet of sentiment and selflessness. Role-model status is a bit of a peculiar goal to be coaxing young lovers drunk on secluded ardour to aim for, but since this sort of thing is catnip for the achievement-oriented, it should give the birth rate a bit of a boost.

'So, your wages are paid by . . . ? Who? The government?'

'No, bank employees. Those who opt in take a pay cut, and that percentage of their wage goes to us, in exchange for a guaranteed match, after which everything usually gets less expensive anyway, on account of sharing bills a few months down the line.'

'Hmmm,' said Milica. 'I don't see how it's possible to make a living this way when there are already dating apps and things like that.'

'The apps don't have the authority to certify couplehood.'

'So?'

'It just makes everything less messy if you have a document that narrows your agreement to commit down to the very hour.'

'How? Pitch it to me as if I'm a prospective client.'

On autopilot, I recited one of the FAQ responses we'd all memorised during training: 'Couplehood certification helps with the paperwork for visas, citizenship, divorce and, last but not least, that state award I mentioned requires documentation that goes back as far as the first date. You can't really put together a satisfying multimedia presentation without these details.'

'Something's still telling me you're pulling my leg,' Milica said. 'I used to think I could imagine an infinitude of dishonest ways of making a living, but what you do never crossed my mind. No offence to you, but I plan on fact-checking all this stuff you've told me when I get home. Do you have business cards, or what?'

My Team Mácha cards are always within easy reach. I handed her one. Milica held it up to the light and squinted as if inspecting a watermark.

'So, according to you, that "someone for everyone" saying is nothing but facts, eh?' she said.

'Yes.'

'What about you? Who's your someone?'

I said 'What?' and, mimicking my voice but making me sound much dumber, Milica said 'Huh?'

I started sweating; I'm not sure why. Could it be that a certain level of rudeness puts pressure on the glands?

'I'm currently unpartnered,' I said, quickly passing a paper napkin over my forehead and hoping she didn't register my dabbing motions.

'By choice?' Milica asked. (The sweat must have escaped her notice; if she'd seen it, she'd have made sure she said something about it.)

'Not exactly, but also in many ways, yes? This is – can we—'

'I wouldn't engage the services of a matchmaker who is herself unmatched,' Milica said, giving her coffee a brisk stir before widening her eyes at me: 'Would you?'

'It depends. Context isn't everything, but it is the main thing, isn't it. Let's . . . er . . . weren't you about to tell me about losing your friend?'

'Ah, yes. How to begin. It wasn't an inevitable change, not like retirement has been . . .'

This is what Milica told me: she trained as a plumber, and stuck to that for the entirety of her working life. The hours suited her. Fiction was what she lived for, but plumbing paid the bills. She wrote when she had ideas and went out on call when she didn't. Her friendships were varied, but only one – the most enduring – was with a fellow plumber, a man named Branko. They'd met during their apprenticeship days. He was the same age as her and, conversationally, what you saw was what you got with Branko – he was a solid person you could talk and laugh with in a relaxed way. They watched TV together, went for early-morning runs, met for brunch, occasionally went on protest marches and picketed parliament. Branko sometimes teased Milica about her literary ambitions, but mostly he was nice about them. He read what she wrote and offered feedback, some of it helpful, but they couldn't agree on what made a story a story, where to locate glee in a sentence, or which tunnels words travel along when written in earnest. A tiresome buffoon began to pop up in the stories Milica wrote. This character was a chronic seeker of cheap metaphors – the type who'd look at the shoots sprouting from

a potato and say 'Ah, now *you* are an indictment of national-
ism.' Milica named this character Branko – which seemed to
amuse the Branko who read her stories. And things continued
that way for a long while – almost a decade, in fact – Milica's
stories grew more and more insulting, and her reader's reactions grew blither and blither. She sometimes felt uneasy about
it, as if on some level the Branko she knew was disappearing
to make way for the caricature she was so busy creating. But
Branko wasn't disappearing; he was merely rallying. One day
about six years ago, right at the end of Dry February, Branko
turned up on Milica's doorstep with a hefty wodge of paper.
Hundreds of printed pages. Writing had filled the time he'd
usually have spent drinking, and now he was ready to be giv-
en a taste of his own medicine. He urged Milica not to pull
any punches with her criticism, but she'd already made up her
mind to encourage him, not demoralise him. Preparing herself to make all manner of charitable allowances, she sat down
for a dutiful hour with Branko's manuscript the same afternoon he handed it over – and she read until dawn. Branko,
Branko whose entire poetic repertoire consisted of football
chants, had written a romance set at the court of an imaginary
Ottoman sultan. The lovers, a court jester and a lion-tamer,
successfully conspired to turn the palace inside-out for just
one night – the final night of both their lives.

'Oh my God,' I said. 'Your friend wrote . . . ?'

'We're not friends any more,' Milica said. 'I couldn't – I
mean, after I finished reading there were a couple of ghastly
hours when I lay on my stomach feeling like I might have to go

to the hospital. But it wasn't anything medical, just common-or-garden fury. I write and write and write for years and don't come up with anything that meets my own standards, let alone Branko's, and then that fucker turns out to have this head full of meteor showers, none of which he EVER so much as hinted at, not even in passing?'

As soon as Milica was able to sit upright again, she saw what needed to happen. Branko had to be dropped, and she, Milica, had to leave the country and start again. She posted Branko's manuscript back to him, packed all her things, then visited a last-minute flight-bookings website and sorted destinations in order of least expensive one-way ticket. She left for Czechia without returning any of that dreadful man's calls or respond-ing to any of his anxious messages asking how she'd liked his pages. 'And then, Kinga – then he went and did this . . .' Milica took me into the bookshop across the street, we found a copy of *A Tale Told by No One to No One* and she showed me the dedication in the front:

For Milica J, who gets her cake and stamps on it

This is so very far from fair, I thought. And: *Fuck this guy*, I thought. This guy who got into another person's stories and made them answer only to him. 'I'm here for you, Milica,' I said. 'Every Monday, at any rate.' I put my arm around my new friend and gave her a strong squeeze – and I suppose the fatal flaw there was due to the hug being more anti-Branko than it was pro-Milica + Kinga. I had to get to work after that, and everything was just as usual. I think I already told you about comparing news alerts with Eva . . .

I met up with Milica again at lunchtime; quite an awkward situation, actually. I arrived at the restaurant to find that she'd also invited her son's girlfriend, Zdenka. It was rainy – not the fine, smooth grey that slips over the city and singes the edges of anything bronze or gold – this rain was more like scrunched-up mud. And mud is already scrunched-up material! I'd rather have had lunch at my office desk. But I'd been summoned via SMS, and, mindful of this being the only day of the week I can be here for her, I came out and sat across from Milica and the shapely divorcee she'd brought along. The small talk was quite frankly rebarbative. Milica would tell me an impressive attribute of Zdenka's, then she'd tell Zdenka something admirable about me, talking quickly so neither of us had time to say more than 'Oh!' or 'Wow, kudos.' What was Milica up to; were we auditioning for the part of daughter-in-law or what? Milica told Zdenka that I speak three languages fluently, and then she told me that Zdenka has a multi-year winning streak on Wordle in English *and* Czech. Zdenka's got a lot of generous and talented friends, and Milica took great care to name and describe the maker of every accessory Zdenka had on that day. I gave Zdenka and Milica a thumbs-up while Milica rushed to defend me against some detractor that only she seemed able to hear – something about me being a person who makes my own way even though I could easily rely on all kinds of showbiz contacts. Alright, alright. I just wanted to eat my soup. What am I whining about, really? Nobody interfered with my lunch; I even got to listen to a rhapsody free of charge. The theme: Zdenka's sportiness. When Zdenka's not skiing, she's swimming, when she's not swimming, she's playing badminton, etc. 'Wonderful,' I said. 'Outstanding,' Zdenka said with a smile, and, as soon as Milica's gaze left her, she laid two fingers against her temple and mimed blowing her own brains out. Keeping a straight face was tricky after that. Milica was smirking too as she harassed us with her praise. And she sped it all up, exhibiting the upbeat anxiety of a bully who only has a few seconds left to inflict trauma before the teacher arrives. She still had to breathe in between salvos, though, and at one such juncture Zdenka proved her mental agility by blurting out 'But that's enough about us, Milica – what have you been up to lately? I hear you've taken to modelling for life-drawing classes in the evenings? How are you finding that?'

Milica blinked, blinked and blinked again until she found just the right variety of spite to inject into her response – something too subtle to pinpoint. The valiant Zdenka retorted, Milica rebuffed the retort . . . and the miracles my new friend attributed to me began to get really interesting. What do I mean by 'interesting'? Well, her statements just kept getting further and further away from the truth. Quite revealing that such a correlation exists for me, but nobody's perfect, right? Besides, I didn't let on that I was interested in what was being said. I spooned up my *kulajda* and, as far as anybody else could see, I remained at the table as a mere corporeal form with all its faculties drenched in dill-infused cream. That last information-missile of Milica's, the one about me being a masseuse, was such a big lie that it really called into question everything Milica had just said about Zdenka, and I mean everything. As in, was Zdenka even involved with Milica's son, and was Milica a mother at all? The marvellous son had been invited to lunch too, but sent his excuses and stayed away. I didn't even get to see who it was Milica was trying to make us compete for. 'Good vibes only,' Milica said, by way of farewell. She said it in English, presumably so that telling us how to feel would have a bit less of a totalitarian flavour than it would have otherwise. Her intonation was indistinguishable from the 'Peace be with you's that get said at Mass; I responded with a 'Good vibes only' of my own before I realised what I was saying. Hearing that must've made Zdenka feel like she had to say it too or out herself as an apostate: 'Good vibes *only.*' And there we had it, thrice confirmed.

I walked back to the office. Rain splattered my umbrella in torpid blobs, but the air had crisped up, and breathing in was like having my nostrils tickled with a fresh lettuce leaf.

In the afternoon, Team Mácha finalised details of the matchmaking mixer we'll be hosting next week. Responses to a survey we sent out indicate that our matchmaking needs to factor in a greater semblance of free will, so now we've got to throw a bunch of our precious charges together and engineer scenarios that entice them to choose the ones we've already established would be a good fit. You tell people that they should go on a date based on data we've gathered concerning shared values, aspirations, adaptation to biographical circumstances and Myers–Briggs personality types, and they find it unsexy. But if, partway through a low-key networking gathering, a pair of attendees stumble into shared custody of a bookshop for two and a half hours (the ideal length of time for a first date) suddenly the spark is there. This sort of thing increases our workload tenfold, but next Friday's mixer has the potential to exceed the cost-to-value ratio of our previous successes by an unquantifiable magnitude. Bonding for the purposes of attaining an extremely short-term goal is fulfilling for our clients and for the employees who endeavour to serve them. It's practice for long-term teamwork that validates our compatibility-assessment skill at the same time as it satisfies the clients' need to identify personality-based attraction as an unexpected guest. These are the claims I made in my preparatory report, anyway. I had to keep taking breaks to battle an intrusive thought: *I've made a mistake.* Not a work mistake. Milica. I shouldn't have drunk coffee with her or eaten lunch with her, I shouldn't have told that person anything, I shouldn't have agreed to replace the friend she'd nurtured with her disdain. I almost want to say that it's unlike me to begin a week this way, but *is* it? Or is this just my usual avid participation in any game that involves meeting somebody else's preferred criteria? The thing I dread began to happen – I unglued my gaze from middle-distance yet could not keep it from returning there; words formed a bucket of sound around me and my responses rattled around in rusty hollows – I could tell from the way the others looked at each other that my replies weren't making much sense. I left the office at half past five, and all the way home I kept wanting to ask Dr Hol's advice. Setting things right, that's where my happiness lies, that's what Mondays are for. I want to be a fixer of mistakes, not a maker of them, but I can no longer ignore Dr H's warning that refusing to be a person who ever does anything wrong is likely to lead to irredeemable error. I called the Doc as soon as I got in, and I told him about my potential mistake. I was afraid I'd be scolded, but he said he was glad I called, and he told me not to be afraid to fall from whatever pedestal I've been placed on.

'But about Milica,' I said.

'Yes. Milica. Tell me why you accepted her overtures despite suspecting her to be an evil person?'

'Did *I* tell you that? That I think Milica might be evil?'

'Yes, you did,' Dr Holý said. 'Just a second ago.'

Is that what I think? I suppose so; otherwise I wouldn't have said it.

Or would I.

Oh no. The middle-distance split and re-joined, split and re-joined.

'Um. It seems like Milica gives me some sort of . . . permission?'

'Permission? What is it that you want or need permission to do?'

'To wonder,' I said, adding, 'I think,' as a potential escape route.

'Alright. Permission to wonder about what?'

'About opposites. About the terrible despair of trying to do what's right, of seeking it out, never to be embraced by goodness in the end – not really. Not to mention the exhaustion of resisting what's wrong.'

'You're feeling exhausted, Kinga-A?' I could hear that Dr Holý was cleaning his glasses.

'Not particularly. I was only trying to tell you what Milica's causing me to wonder about. I can see that she's a bit cruel and . . . I can see that there are other things about her that might offset the spitefulness? If that's true, is it so very different from meeting a really kind person who has issues that make them a horrendous influence on everybody else?'

'Tell me more about this horrendously kind person, Kinga-A. Does anyone in particular come to mind?'

'Not really. Lots of people are kind, and everyone still finds a way to hurt each other all the same, don't they? Oh, hang on – do you know what, never mind all that. We may be arriving at the truth of the matter . . . I think I wanted to be friends with Milica because I had it in the back of my mind that it's good to know somebody with advanced plumbing skills. Just in case.'

'Ho ho,' said Dr Holý. (As far as I can tell, this is what he says instead of laughing. This, or something equally alienating: 'I find that amusing.' I keep meaning to bring those reactions up with him. Are they his way of taking the piss? But then I just chicken out.) 'Anything else?'

'Maybe fraternising with Milica was a way of securing a memento of this day,' I offered. 'You know, after preparing so long. It was good for a moment, actually. The feeling that there was someone I was supposed to meet on this day. No matter what happened in our lives before, and no matter

what happens afterwards, this tiny bit of our fates is identical
. . . starting out as citizens within minutes of each other, you
know?'

Dr H started to say something, but it got difficult to hear
him. Someone was having a full-on coughing fit. Not him, but
someone nearby.

'Has there been somebody else there with you the whole
time?' I asked, almost unable to believe my ears. Like – what
about privacy, what about discretion?

Dr Holý was silent for so long that I thought he'd hung up.
'Hello? Hello?'

'I'm still here, Kinga-A. I just . . . I'm actually on my own in
this room, and I'm also wondering what aspect of our inter-
actions have undermined your confidence in my—'

'Are you telling me you didn't just hear someone coughing
like mad?'

'Of course I heard that,' Dr H said, cleaning his glasses
again.

'You . . . then . . . what—?'

The coughing started again – accompanied by spluttering. I
jumped up off the sofa so fast the phone almost dropped from
my hand. The sounds I was hearing were coming from the
pantry. OUR pantry.

'Dr Holý,' I whispered. 'What should I do?'

'Call the police,' he whispered. 'Should I call them now?'

'Maybe – maybe in a moment or two,' I said. 'Hang on—'

He did. He stayed on the line while I grabbed the biggest
knife I had, slammed my elbow down on the handle of the

pantry door and ran into that windowless room shrieking. The scene should have been ransack and ruin – I mean, that's what I was expecting to find – tins, boxes and jars pushed aside to make room for the Luxury Enamel Posse's trademark suitcase. But everything was arranged in more-or-less perfect order. Except for a silhouette squirming against the far wall. I switched the light on, and the problem sprang very clearly into view – the armchair squeezed in between the shelves, and the man tied to the armchair in an attitude of enforced leisure: head back, arms zip-tied together, legs too. He'd been gagged, but had managed to work the knots loose, or chewed through them, who knew what – now he was panting and coughing with the gag flapping around under his nose.

'WHO ARE YOU?' I screamed. 'WHAT DO YOU WANT?'

The man brought his coughing to a sudden halt. 'Sorry,' he said. 'I tried to be quiet, but I feel like it suddenly got dustier in here.' Then he looked up at me. 'Do you really want to know what I want? Well, let's start with that knife.' This request was made with a great deal more husky yearning than I was able to process, and I backed away fast.

Dr Holý said: 'Kinga-A? What's going on?'

'The knife, Kinga-Alojzia.' The man in the armchair gave me what must surely be a madman's smile, utterly inviolate and dissolute to the core, a super-solstice of a smile that set something like a metronome going inside my head: click, click, click, what, the, fuck. 'I want it,' he said. 'Badly. And I'm going to get it, aren't I?'

What, the, what, the, what, the, I managed a feeble 'No', and he pushed harder: 'Come, light of my eyes. I'm here, you're here, our knife is here, what more do we need? We're ready. Climb on top of me, straddle me well, my murderer, and sink it in. Stab me *here*—' what-the-what-the, he looked down at a point on his left side, below the ribs and above the navel – 'with everything you've got. And don't forget to twist the handle afterwards. Haha – oh my God . . . now that you've finally understood that I was only joking you're starting to look like a competent stabber. How about putting the knife away?'

I set it down on top of a box of pickle jars, handle first, and put the phone on loudspeaker. Which isn't an ethical transgression if the patient does it to the doctor, right?

'So . . . there's a man here,' I told Dr H.

I didn't have to say anything about the man's seeming inability to take it in earnest that he was (probably?) my prey. Dr Holý had already gathered that much: 'But who is he?'

'Who are you?' I asked, for the second time.

Our guest lifted his bound arms and let them flop down again, a madman no longer – now he was all abashed. 'I'm your doctor, Kinga-A. Yes, it's me . . . Dr Holý. I'd really like to talk over the factors that led to this situation at some point, but for now my main goal is getting out of this chair. Could we make that happen?'

I hesitated. I did hesitate. Because I have only ever spoken to Dr Holý on the phone. I might have been lost if not for the fact that I still had Dr Holý on the line, and the Doc was very unhappy to hear somebody claiming to be him. For the first

31

time in, what, twelve years, I heard our doctor raise his voice: 'You're not Dr Holý, *I'm* Dr Holý! Who the fuck are you? Why are you saying you're Dr Holý . . . I mean, me – why are you saying you're me?'

The man in the armchair listened to this with his eyes on the ceiling, and seemed to find a source of equanimity there, because after coughing a couple more times, his rejoinder was mild: 'Alright, alright. You're Dr Holý. Don't get hysterical.'

'Do you really not know who this person is?' Dr Holý asked me. 'How can he be so impudent?'

I began to tell the Doc I'd never seen this man in my life, but paused to take a closer look at my guest so I could be certain that this answer was truthful. Girls, I regret to inform you that this man is . . . um. Mouthwatering. And here's how I see this issue: susceptibility to the beauty of a woman and susceptibility to the beauty of a man are expressions of the difference between moon worship and sun worship. Moving in accordance with the moon, all and any ailments slip loose, you are well, all that you think and feel is translucent. Correspondence with the sun brings an ailment in. Objectification may be the ailment, it may just be a symptom of the ailment, whatever, I looked at the man in the armchair, and for a minute or so I went under, saying to myself, oh no. Black hair that coils back into a ponytail, heavy black eyebrows, a black, black, close-cropped beard for slowly smiling into. Those darknesses of his were like visual absinthe, their tint pitched to such depths that shades of green stirred there. Upsettingly long-lashed, amber-coloured eyes. No, honey-coloured.

No, amber. Actually, I advise you not to look for any closure regarding the colour of his eyes; it's so obvious that they're an aesthetic ambush. He could be a tawnier-skinned Magyar man, or a man of the Caucasus, the lines of his face ever-so-slightly barbed by cataclysmic fluctuations of temper. And is he otherwise well formed? Yes, he stands seven to eight inches taller than us, but the supple bulk of him would be a lot of fun to climb, and, look, I need to return to rationality, so I'll just say good luck with that, girls. 'That' being maintaining decent behaviour around this person. Welcome to your Olympiad of self-control. If I had to guess at who he is socially, I'd say he's a senior software developer. I know I say that about anyone who looks older than thirty, wears a smartwatch and goes around in neutral-coloured hoodie and slacks (or whatever those trousers are supposed to be) but seven and a half times out of ten I'm right, and this is my way of trying to tell you that this man doesn't look like someone I'd be brainy enough to lure into my lair even if I'd wanted to. Which I wouldn't have, because I'm the Kinga who stays in my mistake-fixing lane, remember?

'I've never seen this man before,' I told Dr Holý.

'Well, of course – if you say so,' said the man in the armchair. 'That version works for me too. Just untie me – you do realise that tying me up was a criminal act? Let me go right now, I'll suddenly have no idea who you are either, and we'll say no more about it.'

'He's tied up?' That was Dr Holý again. 'Are you – going to untie him?'

'I'm not sure,' I said. 'You sound like you think I shouldn't. I was actually going to, until he claimed to be you.'

'Yeah, no, those second thoughts are fair,' the man in the armchair said. 'That was kind of a suspicious thing to do. But I'm not going to say I shouldn't have done it, because if you hadn't been talking to "Dr Holý", it probably would've worked.'

'You can't say "Dr Holý" like that, he actually is Dr Holý,' I said.

The man in the armchair shrugged. 'Hope that's true!'

'Is it starting to feel as if tying him up was – perhaps not the right thing to do, per se, but, you know . . . necessary?' Dr Holý asked.

'You're *amazingly* unprofessional,' the man in the armchair said to Dr Holý, then to me: 'Just untie me. Pretty please.'

Kinga-Blažena, as you will very soon see once you take over tomorrow, I decided against that. Telling Dr Holý I'd call him back, I sat down on the floor. Not close enough to the chair to make any sudden movements worth my guest's while, but close enough to really look at him and reflect upon both his intentions and the intentions of the one who'd tied him up. He knew our name, and knew that we were in frequent contact with a Dr Holý. He might even know that Dr H is a psychiatrist.

Beware, girls. The man in the armchair knows plenty. As soon as he saw that Dr Holý had hung up, he called out 'Siri 112! Siri sto dvanáct, Siri sto dvanáct, Siri sto dvanáct,' until he was forced to accept that he was never going to be faster than the person who actually had the phone in her hand and could make sure Siri failed to complete dialling the number for emergency services every time. Finally, sounding like the most aggrieved of the aggrieved, our guest said: 'I have excretory needs. Can you find it in your heart to let me attend to those?'

He says his name's Jarda.

I returned the knife to the kitchen, then went into the bedroom, brought my copy of Wisława Szymborska's *Selected Poems* out from under our pillow and got Jarda to place his hand on it and swear he wouldn't try anything if I helped him up. He swore, and was true to his word – shuffled to the bathroom and back with a martyr's resignation. I've questioned and questioned him, and he has shifted strategies, starting off by answering my questions with the question 'Who do you think I am?' and switching to 'I'll tell you everything when you untie me.' After about half an hour of that, he stopped making any verbal response whatsoever and simply stared at me. Were I in this Jarda's position, I think I'd opt for reticence too. Claiming to be Dr H didn't work today, but something else might work tomorrow, so why not sleep on it, right?

He should be fine for the night. He was fed *pierogi* and had a couple of shots of vodka before I locked him in for the night. I don't think he's asleep yet. A few minutes ago, I pressed an ear to the pantry door and he's murmuring phrases to himself, the same phrase altered slightly each time he says it. Practising for tomorrow, I expect.

My darlings, it's no secret that the day you voted me squad leader was the happiest day of my life. We were all deserving

– each one of us could have taken on Mondays and crushed them. But you chose me. You lifted me up on your shoulders as the one to set the tone for our entire week, and on that day, I vowed to become worthy of the esteem you'd shown me. Some Mondays I've made that happen – I'm certain of it. Other Mondays . . . well. No matter which way I think about it, the current situation is one that's developed on my watch, and I'm sort of in shock that I've let us down this badly.

For a number of months . . . OK, for close to a year, our weekly schedule hasn't been completed as we agreed. I have not only noticed that, but glossed over it in my diary entries. I had an idea that one of us was a little restless and would either settle down in due course or reach out requesting that we make a change. She hasn't.

I thought there was safety in numbers, safety in the fact that there are six of us and one of her. I'm no longer confident that we have any meaningful advantage over her. My silence added steel to her nerve, and even if she began with some intention of negotiating, that spirit of compromise is long gone.

I'll start with this:

Look at the calendar.

Observe that it'll be our name day on 3 March . . . this Sunday. That's right: Cunigunde, the Saint and Empress whose name ours is a version of, died on that day in 1033. You're shrugging; we don't do *svátek*s. The celebration of Babcia's name day was a matter of diplomacy (aka survival). That was the only *svátek* we bothered with. What of Cunigunde of Luxembourg, then – what did we know about her? She was one of the most powerful rulers of the eleventh century. All that and she was a good person, too – super pure in thought and action. That was it, there was no need to ask anything else. We didn't rate Cunigunde of Luxembourg at all, and might have gone for another name when we got old enough. Except that in secondary school, our Religious Education teacher asked the class if anybody had heard about the fight St Cunigunde had with her niece Judith. No . . . what fight? And who was Judith? Oh, Judith was a negligent abbess. Her sisters in Christ cried out for guidance while she made the rounds at parties. One of Judith's forsaken nuns asked Cunigunde to have a word, and Cunigunde obliged – she sat down with her niece and clearly told her she was making a mockery of the Holy Vows she'd taken, but that it wasn't too late to honour the Vows and lead her flock along the Path to Righteousness. Abbess Judith convincingly presented herself as a chastened listener, lowering her gaze, making repentant noises – but immediately went out to another party. And another, another. The Abbess didn't go home for three days, but when she finally did return to the nunnery, her Aunty Cunigunde was waiting. Cunigunde hadn't lost her temper – but she did understand that it wasn't possible for words to convey her message. So instead of saying anything else, she gave Abbess Judith such a hard slap that the finger-marks remained on Judith's face for the rest of her life.

There's a tiny face people occasionally pull after I've told them my first name. Many seem to think they've managed to hide their reaction with words that are nice-nice and fake polite, but I always catch it. The expression says: *Oh, you've just found the most concise way to tell me you're that woman who takes your enormous hoop earrings off and puts them in an inner pocket of your tracksuit before you and your friends jump someone outside McDonald's because she's obviously got a death wish, there can't be any other reason she opened that dumb mouth of hers to speak to YOUR MAN. Even more insane of her to promise you that YOUR MAN is no prize and she was only asking if he was going in or leaving because he was standing in her way like a boulder of oblivion . . .*

I see that little face, and, oh, if only I was that Kinga, *pow pow*, upfront and direct. Instead I have my own 'well, aren't you trashy' face to pull in return. Especially after hearing that someone's been named after a saint who got canonised after martyrdom or healing people . . . *That's hardly paradigm-shifting stuff, is it, love?* St Kinga, on the other hand . . . St Kinga isn't about being subjected to agony or taking other people's pain away. She hurt someone and made it holy. OK, I do remember that the Religious Education teacher seemed worried about that interpretation of what she'd said, and tried to make the whole thing a bit more morally sound by mentioning crises that Heaven forced St Cunigunde to endure at other times in her life. But placed alongside the forever slap, Cunigunde's dolorous trials crumble into dust. Girls, we're our Babcia's granddaughter, so there was never any way for us to avoid being named after a saint. Cunigunde was a better choice than most.

Now I feel an overwhelming desire to be named after a

saint whose feast day is in December or something. Sunday is too close.

This year, 3 March will be the day Cunigunde does one more saintly deed – she's planning to drive out the demons.

What demons, you may ask.

Us. We're the demons! A convenient construct. Getting rid of six demons makes her less of a psycho than getting rid of six other Kingas does.

Think there's been a misunderstanding of some sort? I wish. How I wish.

Let's review the weekly schedule.

As agreed, Mondays are mine.

Kinga-Blažena gets us through Tuesdays in the manner of her choice. And you choose cynicism, Kinga-B. Let's see – how does this go:

1. When the chips are down nobody actually gives a shit about each other.
2. Everyone's a liar, everything's a scam.
3. You only do a favour to call in a favour later.
4. You're nobody's fool, and you'll openly repay any insult in full.

What have I missed out? Plenty, I'm sure. I just don't have your knack for negative thinking. Since this isn't the time to start another back-and-forth re: self-fulfilling prophecies, I'll take this chance to express gratitude for your help at work instead. You could've worked with Kinga-C instead, but you heeded the call to bring lonely people together. Look, I'm not expecting you to relate to my feeling of being a staunch foot soldier in True Love's battalion. I just want everyone to find a haven in the arms of someone who'll do their utmost not to hurt them! Do you think I don't realise how ambitious that is? It's enough that you consider matchmaking gainful employment in some – any – way. I haven't thanked you enough for spending your time the way you do . . . and I'm thanking you now.

Kinga-Casimira gets Wednesdays. Kinga-C, I feel like you have some sort of questionnaire for existence that's getting completed Wednesday by Wednesday. You strike me as the only one of us who fully relies on the people around you, and maybe also the only one who can be fully relied on by others. You never seem to have Plan B, C, and/or D ready, but you've managed to stay alive this way for so long that there must be more than just luck involved here. Could you be carrying the lion's share of our intuition? If I find that some body part is bruised, dislocated or sprained when Monday comes around, I go straight to your section of the diary to find out what happened. Beloved weirdo, I can only hope it feels like you're getting the answers you were looking for.

On Thursdays Kinga-Duša attends the various appointments Kinga-B and I book, delivering herself into the hands of others with unquestioning serenity. We all know how to be still – that's the main reason this agreement of ours retains functionality – but Kinga-D, your stillness is more regal than ours. You seem more fulfilled by it, more capable of perceiving it as an end in itself. That's why we place ourselves in your hands in turn, and leave maintenance day to you. You're such a well-hydrated, unbothered queen. It's thanks to you that we still appear to be in full bloom. Bright eyes, nails, teeth and so on. When I look in the mirror, a woman with a dirty chuckle looks back. You can see it in her smile lines . . . wryness runs along its appointed tributaries. Glee, too.

Kinga-Eliška, Fridays are yours. Thanks for at least signing for packages in the morning before you drift away into the clouds. No, that isn't how I want to talk to you – I'll try again. What is it that makes me squint so much over the way you account for Fridays . . . it could be the gluttony I find there? Not gluttony towards anything that can be held or touched or more deeply recognised over time. No, it's for shadows, or images, or echoes. I can't work out what you think real life is supposed to be. And I can't work out why you're with us. You once wrote to me that if the two of us ever met, we wouldn't be friends. We wouldn't even be friendly. All of that is true, and yet. On my way out of the door this morning, I grabbed a book, *The Devil's Larder*, to read on the tram. And as I turned the pages, reading, I began to feel full. You'd marked your place in the book with a spritz of perfume. You must have done that weeks ago; the oil had trickled all the way through the wood pulp and your place in the text was lost. But the bound paper had become something hot and cold at once. The pages fanned my face and fed me the pulpy seeds melting a mound of cream-flecked ice: a big spoonful of pomegranate *bingsu* and a small sip of matcha; I felt the acid blush of that on my tongue, and for a zeptosecond, if that, I was gripped by some sort of *sensation reversed*? As if the book had just shown me what it's like to be read. Because of you I can cross over sometimes, think things I don't think I think, and believe things I don't believe I believe. You're like a riddle that vouches for me whenever I'm confronted by some sphinx-like corner of what I see or hear.

Kinga-Filoména plays our Saturdays by ear, pleased with and satisfied by all that falls under 'just because'. Sometimes I think that really the rest of us are working for your sake, we're working for a single day of the week that's conducted without ulterior motives. It's not that I think you owe us an in-depth commentary of that miraculous day; you're well within your rights on the Saturdays when you only bother to record two words: *Solitary brooding!* But I perk up when you tell us that the world's tiniest water lily is back in bloom, and you've been to see it at the greenhouse in Troja. As for your claim that the water lily's favourite piece of music is *The Lark Ascending*: OK, if you say so. Then, once in a while, I blush all the way through an entry where you tell us about a spree of uninhibited move- ment – dancing, fucking, or both – stuff I really like in theory but experience as terror when I try to put them into practice. There are too many ways to get left behind, locked out, miss a turning point in the rhythm and never rediscover the part that felt like it came naturally. But you . . .

Three or four Mondays ago, someone sent me a video of you. This sometimes happens to me while I'm scrutinising our boys' and girls' posts, likes and comments to round out Team Mácha's assessments of their love languages and attachment styles. Thanks to the omnipotence of People You May Know suggestions, my work gets interrupted by people who've met you – it's always you they're trying to contact, Kinga-F, never any of the others. This video was from a member of a stag party that accosted you on the street, lifted you up in the air and ran down to the riverbank singing a drinking song. One of the lads must have hung back a little bit to film it all: it looks as if they've caught you on your way back from the corner shop. You're not dressed for a party. You've got a coat thrown on over your pyjamas, but that doesn't stop you from accepting the invitation. You settle onto that boy's broad shoulders as if they were created for the purpose of transporting you around town. You swing your legs, wave your arms and command your steed to run faster – he does, and so does the rest of the herd. You're singing along with them despite not knowing a word of the Dutch language, you're making do with *neh-nah-nah*s and *la la la*s. Your tongue doesn't twist, you don't lower your voice, there's no trailing away. In this video, as you alternate between singing and shouting GIDDY UP, you swig from a wine bottle that's confiscated by the nearest stag-party member and promptly handed back because – he turns to the camera with a dumbfounded look – *it's non-alcoholic*. It's probably your being like that whilst sober that created a need in this young man. A need to track you down and reach out. Thinking that I was you, he asked me to be his wedding date. I blocked him without sending a reply. Let him keep looking for you; some people need a search like that to get themselves organised.

Now we come to Sunday, the day of rest. Kinga-Genovéva's

day. She did say that was what she was going to do with her day. Sleep in, unplug from the news and any sense of obligation to reply to messages, take baths, click and scroll through some pop culture. Sounds great. I'd have been even more of a fan of spending Sundays this way if she'd offered to do just a little bit of laundry too; then I wouldn't be the only person who ever sees to it that textiles are washed and folded around here. Just saying. Aside from that, I did always feel ready to jump straight into Monday's tasks when Kinga-G really had been resting on Sundays. When she switched from resting to praying, I felt the difference immediately.

Almost a year ago – on 6 March 2023, in fact, I woke up with a rosary wound around the fingers of my right hand and a King James Bible clutched to my chest with my left hand. There was a bookmark stuck in the bible, and when I opened it up, there was Matthew 12:43–45, vehemently underlined. Yes, the 'seven unclean spirits' passage:

43:When the unclean spirit is gone out of a man, he walketh through dry places, seeking rest, and findeth none.

44:Then he saith, I will return into my house from whence I came out; and when he is come, he findeth it empty, swept, and garnished.

45:Then goeth he, and taketh with himself seven other spirits more wicked than himself, and they enter in and dwell there: and the last state of that man is worse than the first. Even so shall it be also unto this wicked generation.

Shots fired. I laughed it off at first, though. I just thought, come on, if this is really what our Sunday Girl is up to, wouldn't she be craftier? Wouldn't that Kinga-G dissemble until the very last minute and then annihilate the rest of us without warning?

But then, on a whim of sorts, I checked Google Maps on our phone. Kinga-G had been to Mass. I was immediately shown the walking directions to and from St Jiljí's in Old Town. And the fitness-tracker phone showed me the corresponding step count and timeframe. St Jiljí's offers a Polish-language Mass at noon, but get this, girls: Kinga-G goes to the 6:30 p.m. Czech-language mass. This is a woman on a mission to start afresh. She's dropping the language of her Baptism, First Holy Communion and Confirmation, and intends to pray in the language of her new country. She goes to Mass, and then she goes for walks in the parkland surrounding Bohnice Psychiatric Hospital. Fucking long walks. This is what our phone tells me. She's been doing all this, and her diary entries have never changed. *Stayed in bed, caught up on TV.*

Yeah, right. I bet this is what she'd have us believe; that this man fell out of our TV screen. Probably while she was watching a show about exorcists. You might not think an exorcist would lie about being Dr Holý, but today's been jam-packed with stuff I didn't see coming, so nothing is a given here.

I've been keeping a broken candle in the bottom drawer of our bedside table for six months or so. I don't know if you've noticed it; it's a tapered gold baton that looks whole as long as you handle it with delicacy. It wobbled when I set it upright in the candlestick. Now that the candle is standing, it's inclined to separate along the fissure that sits exactly halfway between the taper and the base. It wobbled, yet held together. I've lit the candle – this is something I'm doing in case I don't get another Monday. This is what I wanted to see. I'm lying down now, watching the flame sway and stretch, sometimes towards me, sometimes away from me, scattering gold. I wonder how this candle will burn; I wonder if it can continue forging this dazzling path after I've closed my eyes; I wonder who will wake to see what's left after a broken candle burns through the night.

TUESDAY

Alright, Mses Sikora – welcome to story time with your host, Kinga-Blažena.

Team Mácha's star couple came to the office today: so photogenic, so personable. Frída and Lien. They asked if they could speak to Franta, but Franta was in a meeting with some Profitability Monitor types from HQ.

'Oh . . . then could we see Eva?'

Eva was in the same meeting, and Valérie was off sick. 'We'll just talk to the other one, then,' Lien said. I told them that Pavlína was still finding her feet here and would probably have to consult one of her superiors on anything they discussed with her anyway, so they might as well have this chat with me. They didn't want to, but they knew better than to openly refuse. It's been like this ever since they fully clocked that I'm only nice to them when they're making themselves useful. I probably didn't mention this at the time (as always, a lot of other things were going on) but Frída and Lien's courtship process was playlist-intensive. Those playlists are far and away the most shared content on Team Mácha's website these days. Not that F & L were happy for that content to be posted in the first place. For all their head-turning looks, theirs is an intensely introverted union. *No*, Lien told me, *no no no*, that level of show and tell was never part of the deal. Frída was whining too, *Those playlists are just for us, how did you even find out about them*, blah blah blah. They gave me no choice but to show them some ruthlessness. There were, after all, all sorts of other communications between Frída and Lien that I had discovered and would have no problem spamming their family and friends with. Once they understood their options, they chose common sense. So there's a Polaroid-style photo of Frída alongside her blend of slow jams, sonatas, arias and concertos, and a rose-tinted snap of Lien to go with her choices – classic rock, noise pop and loads of jazz: big band, bebop, fusion and so on. Just look at those faces, valiant in their vulnerability. This is how people with the ability to forge strong and healthy bonds look. But they aren't the only ones. The first song on Lien's playlist for Frída is 'It Could Happen to You'. Awwww. We recommend that listeners work their way through the playlists alternating Frída's picks with Lien's, and in the comments section underneath, romance junkies write about starting to listen with scepticism, then slowly dropping their guard as the pieces tease and then continue each other. Maybe six songs in – three of Frída's selections plus three of Lien's – these wistful eavesdroppers start claiming to hear a harmony that seeps in through the cracks left in centuries and geographies. The Song, the fated Song of Lien and Frída. Amen; this is exactly what's needed to make Team Mácha seem like healers instead of the sticking-plaster merchants we actually are. Too many see being liked or loved as some kind of character reference: *Oh, X seems to enjoy spending time with me, so I can't be too much of a mess. So-and-so seems happy to officially make it known that we're sleeping together on a long-term basis – they'd avoid doing this if I was that bad.*

Hilarious. Most of us actually *are* that bad.

Kinga-C and/or Kinga-E, before you come at me, I'm not ignoring the fact that we come with pleasant characteristics built in too. I just haven't encountered any traits that make up for the tribal mindset, the faddishness, the miserly attention span, the dishonesty whenever honesty matters most, the deep stores of ineffectual empathy, etc. New clients tell me about their hopes of coming across the kind of person they'd be willing to change their ways for, and I'm just like . . . LOL. That's quite the hope. You're calling on affiliation to alter your very nature? You want the so-called love of another person to accomplish a task that religion, military dictatorships, representative democracy and every system in between hasn't managed to do? A matchmaker has only one attainable goal: steering an individual away from enablers of their specific toxic traits and towards another individual with whom quiet coexistence is possible. Getting people spoused up is a damage-limitation exercise from start to finish. Aim any higher than that and you stray into stupidities.

Back to our star couple, Frída and Lien: they resigned as Team Mácha ambassadors today. They started off with a rehearsed revelation: Frída had discovered Lien's infidelity. Lien couldn't apologise enough for the heartache she'd caused, but wasn't really trying to find a way forward that involved staying together. Lien admitted to having a lot to learn about ending a relationship with maturity. Frída nodded, then they shared a hug and wished each other the best. Our former star couple are good liars, resolute. They showed no nerves at all whilst playing sinner and pardoner, but they must not have had that much faith in each other's fibbing skills, because as soon as I made casual mention of the (non-existent) lie detector test they'd need to pass before discharge from promotional duties, truths emerged.

Frída and Lien don't really like each other.

'Oh,' I said. 'You dislike each other?'

'No . . .' Lien said.

They just . . . feel nothing for each other. I asked them to clarify. 'You've been pretending to care about each other? Since when, and to what end?'

'Not pretending,' Frída said. 'We had all the feelings. We just didn't notice that they weren't for each other.'

'OK. If anyone asks, we're just going to say you drifted apart, then.'

'Perfect,' said Lien. 'Can we . . . leave now?'

'In a minute. First I'd like to try to understand if this is something you can work through. With our support, of course.'

A terrified glance flashed between them – a glance that said: Sakra! *She's going to make us stay together until she dies. She's got to be at least fifteen years older than us, though, so at least there's that.*

We went on talking until we met in the middle. I'd thought they were trying to tell me that they'd been idealising each other and had hit a wall with that, but that wasn't it. Their connection was forged on an absence of contradiction. And that was a non-connection, really – they were stimulated by the same sounds, but remained so entirely separate, each relating to the sounds on her own, that these stimuli couldn't even be thought of as a bridge between the two of them, let alone felt as one. People like to act as if love is agreeing on a lot of little things and hate is disagreeing on a few big things, or some version thereof. Excuse me . . . I'm so sorry – believe it or not, this faithful correspondent of yours truly does grieve for our species – but no. These supposed harmonies and dissonances are a weak excuse for emoting all over each other. 'Moonlight Serenade' is playing, and Lien listens – it's more than listening, she hears, she and the notes are one, it's as if Glenn Miller and his band have got all their gear set up in the space where her lungs were and she's breathing out the breeze from their clarinets. 'Moonlight Serenade' plays for Frída, and poor Frída gets carried away as well. Lien stuffed all her 'Moonlight Serenade'-related emotions into an envelope and addressed it to Frída (crossing out the name of the person that very same envelope was previously addressed to) – Frída sent her own sentiment-stuffed envelope to Lien, and somehow the tens, or hundreds, of crossed-out names on these envelopes weren't visible to the latest recipients. Now that they've both seen the light, they don't want to discuss it. Their sheepishness was plain to see. I asked if they'd like be rematched, or if there was any other way Team Mácha could assist.

Lien: 'No, that's OK, I think I'm just going to focus on work from now on.'

Frída: 'Yeah, same.'

As soon as they'd left, Pavlína hurried my way and stood

in front of my desk twisting her hands together, shifting from foot to foot and exhibiting other 'new-found conscience five seconds prior to being busted' mannerisms. 'Did you, um, do you think it was us that broke them up?' she whispered.

I asked her to close the door behind her. She did, and repeated her question. Pavlína's my work daughter. No wife for me – I'm more than happy to leave Eva to Kinga-A. Ugh, Eva who clearly thinks (but doesn't say) that the dodgy and the BRAVE live in Žižkov. If Eva wants to foist her goody-goody news updates on me and get a little dab of something disturbing from me, that's fine. But outside of that dynamic, which I've sustained with Kinga-A's continuity preferences in mind, Eva isn't my kind of woman at all. Pavlína, though . . . she's this restless and overqualified blonde who pounces on our to-do lists with predatory force. Her weakness for being singled out as existing on her own extra-special level of impeccability screams daddy issues, but it was only with maximal exertion that I beat Franta's bid to become her Office Daddy. Franta surprised me, and may even have surprised himself, with the strength of his desire to be the one this twenty-something tigress looks to for approval. He really put up a fight. More of a fight than if we were both trying to date her, actually, thereby revealing himself as the type who vies for control with much more focus than he would ever vie for affection. There were underhand gambits galore. I can't risk putting them down in writing, but I might leave you a voice note with some details later.

Today's chat with my office daughter was all about making

sure she didn't go to Mummy Eva with her concerns – a step she'd only take if she got an idea that my downfall was close at hand and she'd be implicated. But it's handled; I put my protégé on to the idea of her capsizing alone. I reminded her that Frída and Lien partly owed their three years of contented coupledom to us. Pavlína went *Yeah, but.* I asked Pavlína if she thought it was possible for a healthy relationship to be tampered with from the outside. Pavlína went *No, but.*

'But what, Pavlína? Speak up. What is it?'

Pavlína began recalling a Special Project she said I'd requested her aid with. (I'm recording this as a point of information for the four Mses Sikora who don't work for our living.) According to Pavlína, I, 'Kinga Sikora', instructed her to guess the passwords for a number of Lien and Frída's accounts, examine hundreds of pages of messages exchanged between them, set up an e-mail address in Lien's name and another e-mail address in Frída's name, then send a convincing break-up e-mail from 'Lien' to the real Frída, and another break-up e-mail from 'Frída' to the real Lien on the same evening.

Please observe the audacity, the cut-throat opportunism of today's workforce. Colleagues will make accusations like this without even thinking twice.

'Pavlína, this project sounds . . . well, really involved, amongst other things. Why would I or anybody go to such lengths to cause trouble in our star couple's paradise?'

'For the drama,' Pavlína mumbled. 'You said their love needed to be tested, it needed an obstacle to overcome. You said that love has to undergo at least seven trials, and that if

Lien and Frída were able to get through those together, then we'd know we're real matchmakers. Give them a month to get through this, you said, and if they do, we'll set the next test.'

'Hmmm? When was this?'

'You know when. Exactly twenty-two days ago, at full moon!'

Who actually raised Pavlína? It's not just her manner of marking time, but her assumption that everybody else does it this way too. We'll have to get to the bottom of that some other week.

'Last month, you say? Well, I can't wait to see the evidence. You're our cleverest team member. You know how intimidated the others are. I mean, how can you hold two academic degrees already . . . one from Charles University and one from the Sorbonne . . . my goodness. There's no way a cookie that smart would do the things you've just told me about without documentation that proves she wasn't acting on her own initiative, so let's take a look at that together. Times, dates, everything . . . then we can sort out this misunderstanding. Oh, you don't have anything? Then I'll let you go for now, Pavlína. I'm sure you've got a lot to think about.'

Pavlína . . . haha, Pavlína actually slammed the door on her way out. Kinga-A wants to be here, I want to be here, and that's it. The rest of our colleagues are either biding their time until they can leave or they're furtively applying for transfers to other departments that have more of a connection with actual banking. The other week I found Valérie in a full-blown mope on the terrace; between fathoms-deep drags on her cigarette she grieved for the members of Team Mácha, for our talent and our training, both of which she says are being put to 'trivial uses'. How is handling money more serious than matters of the heart and loins, though? Seriously: how? The others seem unwilling to enlighten me on that front; they're all too busy finding ways to hide their belief that they're better than the work they have to do. Eva personalises her desk space and calls it her 'home from home', Franta's making a disturbing collage with lines from thank-you notes we've received. He intends for it to spread all around the office walls. Pavlína's not like us, and she spelled that out by declining the invitation to her own welcome lunch. Seated at her desk just a few metres away from mine, Pavlína hit 'reply all' and announced that she couldn't make it. No 'unfortunately', no 'it was nice of you to organise this', and not even the vaguest allusion to a reason. Franta wrote back asking about other dates that might be more convenient, and Pavlína didn't respond. She's been here for almost a year now and her welcome lunch has become a taboo topic. For a while we all thought Pavlína must have replied to Franta directly, but a couple of months ago I heard Franta asking Valérie if he should try resending his e-mail about alternative dates. If he'd asked my advice, I'd have badgered him to resend the e-mail. And if Pavlína still didn't reply, I'd have gone up to her and said 'Sorry about this, love, but Franta asked me to ask you why you're so ungrateful,' you know, all the stirring requisites for an Ugly Morning at the office. But it was Valérie Franta asked, so she only went pale and whispered 'No . . . leave it, leave it.' What I mean to say here is: Pavlína's confrontation skills have deteriorated due to all this cosseting from our colleagues – *Oooh, Pavlína doesn't want to be welcomed, let's tiptoe around her until it's time to say goodbye* . . . so she got off to a rusty start with that mini-confrontation of hers. But she'll regroup – at least, this is an Office Daddy's affectionate wish. Resilience is key! Needless to say, I'll be ready for her resurgence. And on we go until one of us topples the other.

About the e-mail instance she mentioned . . . if that was anything more than a wild claim Pavlína felt moved to make, Frída and Lien had plenty of chances to name it as their turning point. *She e-mailed me to say it's over and I took it in without sadness or relief* – one or both of them could have told me something like that. I pressed them pretty hard for a definitive instance of disconnection, to no avail. Maybe they made some sort of pact that keeping the particulars of their break-up to themselves would be their parting gift to each other? I may not know much about couplehood, but it does seem jam-packed with oblique diplomacies. (I'm thinking about the way that all attempts to side with one half of a quarrelling couple only serve to unite the combatants against you and teach you the folly of attacking a double-headed creature.)

I'm carrying our notebook around with me today, jotting things down as they occur to me; there's no time to wait for privacy. Just now, Franta asked if I was writing down what he'd just said to me, and without looking up I said 'How would it make you feel if I said "yes", Franta?' and he said 'Nervous and flattered.' Then I asked if he'd like me to show him what

I'd written down. And I'm not going to tell you what he said to that because you'd only skip it anyway. Just as I often do, after all, while he's actually talking.

About this morning . . . I've been simmering over it, but I'll come to it now. And I'm bringing my bone with me. What bone? The one I have to pick with Kinga-Alojzia, who is most unmistakably back on her bullshit this week. My notes will range from least concerning to most concerning, beginning with our classic problem: Kinga-A talks down to us. As far as she's concerned, we're Kinga-A and Her Backing Dancers. She tosses us a few crumbs of 'admiration', I point out what she's doing, and you come after me telling me she means well, she's a seeker of positivity and all the rest of it. Some of the notes our Kinga of Virtue has written to me piss me off so much I read them aloud to Dr Holý, who turns out to be far from impartial, too. Kinga-A is positive and Kinga-B is negative . . . really? Could you get any more simplistic than that? I am weighing up different ways to break this pattern, and one of them is going on strike on Tuesdays. No going in to the office, no responding to Eva's dehydrating messages, no laundry, I'll just lounge around sending gourmet tourists spiralling by creating Tripadvisor listings and rave reviews for restaurants that don't exist. That'll be my sole purpose until Kinga-A pulls her socks up and addresses us as equals. Please indicate whether or not you're willing to back me up by striking on your respective days. Don't let her get away with acting as if she did all the citizenship application prep alone, don't let her get away with claiming the success of that application as meaningful to her alone. You should've seen me in the shower this morning, belting out 'Kde domov můj' with a soapy hand pressed to my heart. I was *happy*. An irrational state, considering the headache that was turning my vision into a Rubik's cube and the danger extravaganza Kinga-A so airily left me in charge of. Seriously: danger, danger, everywhere.

Mses Sikora, I was dreaming (a first-class dream, by the way; a certain person who gets on my nerves was having a terrible day and I got to be an invisible spectator who could occasionally be heard laughing) but then the dream became circular, I was still there but everything I saw was through a porthole frame, then the circle shrank, and I did too, rolling around in a dream the size of a coin, which was then tossed onto a mountain of fluff that turned out to be a pillow. From there the dream became – not exactly what I would call a nightmare, but definitely not as joyous as I'd been finding it; someone was leaning over the pillow and blowing on my face. Their breath was very hot and either smelled like melting leather or was generating that smell as it toasted my skin. Then a blob of something warm dropped onto my forehead and confirmed I wasn't dreaming any more. The unattended candle on the bedside table had to be blown out, wax had to be pulled, peeled and flicked away from hair, and it had to be done at a snail's pace, since my hands were none too steady and vodka was guzzling my blood and munching on my brain like the filthy beast it is. I started our Tuesday sprawled directly beneath a candle that had abandoned the standard behaviour of candles and decided to twist around just as it liked, apparently discovering something analogous to joints and cartilage within its structure as it did so. That small and sputtering flame was bent over me in a weirdly protective way, too. If equipped with the capability to have a verbal go at an intruder, it might have shouted something like: *Hey, numbskull! If you dare try anything with her, you'll have me to deal with first!* Oddly endearing, but not something a Kinga of sound mind can be dwelling on when we've got a living to earn. I also want to note that all this was before I exchanged morning greetings with the MAN Kinga-A had locked up in the pantry. If there are any aspects of Monday that our leader wasn't exaggerating about, he's got to be one of them. 'Man' had to be written in capital letters because he – I mean, how can I say this . . . it's hard to know how feminine one feels on any given day, right? Unless it's a day when physical nearness to someone like that twangs your hormones so hard that you sort of just . . . shake.

Finding someone like that locked up in our pantry got me Thinking.

My theory: something's happened to Kinga-A. A different Kinga must've hijacked Monday. I know all your handiwork too well to imagine that this could be something any of you six would do, so this had to be a Kinga we'd never heard from before. A Kinga-H who's chosen to debut with a bang, making sure we mark our first week as a Czech citizen with an in-depth tour of the prison system. Then I remembered to check our diary, and changed my mind about everything.

I suppose it's still a possibility that it wasn't Kinga-Alojzia who wrote yesterday's diary entry. There is one thing that gives me pause more than the parts where she doesn't quite sound like herself. It's the provenance of this 'transcription', as she called it. The pages were printed out and stuffed into our notebook, thereby concealing the diarist's handwriting. Sus. Even more sus: I can't find the original voice recording that would validate identification of those pages as a transcription. Yesterday's diary entry could have been typed up across an indefinite span of time and printed out when it was time to strike. Or Kinga-A said some things in the voice note that she thought better of and eradicated from the text. There could have been some background noises she didn't want to explain . . . look, I'm more inclined to take the disappearance of the voice recording as Kinga-A behaving exactly like herself, panicking because she feels like she fucked up. Taking credit for resolving situations that were already resolving themselves: that's all Kinga-Alojzia is good for.

Issue number two: the criminalisation of unreported lifestyle changes. Kinga-A wants all behaviours announced at all times, but oh no, Kinga-G tells us she's been lazing about on Sundays when actually she's out praying and probably going for walks with lonely psychiatric patients and who knows what other forms of hideous do-gooding! ST KINGA HAS GOT TO BE STOPPED. And what is this panic based on? Ah yes, a few Bible passages bookmarked by Kinga-G. Only a narcissist pretending to have a guilt complex would find those lines menacing. And of course, Kinga-A doesn't say *how* we stop Kinga-G. It's up to us how we eliminate the threat. Our gentle leader would never suggest ditching Kinga-G first . . . well, not unless consensus was heading in that direction. Alright, but supposing consensus did head in that direction and we ended up suppressing Kinga-G, ask yourselves this: Who would be next on the hitlist?

I'll tell you what – we got the leader we deserve. We let her keep Mondays even after the stunt she pulled. And now she's trying to frame someone else for stuff that so far only she has proved capable of doing. She even referenced it in her entry – a casual taunt. Those three weeks she spent in France quarantining with our brother. Three weeks of Kinga-A all day, every day. If it sounds like I'm getting angry with our big sister for hogging the symptoms of Covid-19, that isn't it at all. I'm not complaining about missing out on a few Tuesdays with Benek, either. Alright, I am complaining about that a little bit. It's Benek after all. But that brother of ours called me on the way to work this morning, he very patiently repeated things he already told a few of you, and if he's in town some Tuesday soon, we'll meet then; it's fine.

No, the main thing is that Kinga-Alojzia mugged us. She ripped our conscious hours away first and apologised afterwards. I don't know how it was for the rest of you. You never really said. I have re-read each of your entries for those weeks that disappeared on us. Livid, perplexed entries that don't go anywhere near the experience of trying to wake up three times and not even managing to get your eyes open. You can't have forgotten how scary she was. She bore down on me so hard, and I struggled like mad, like mad . . . I remember kind of retching, but it was only making attempts at breathing, and she kept bearing down until the notion of oxygen being something worth fighting for had utterly deserted me and I was just like, well, never mind then. Going limp was even more humiliating than wriggling around – I think because her attitude didn't change when she got what she wanted; Kinga-A taking over my day of the week was a 1:1 reproduction of our grandmother wringing a chicken's neck. That's what Kinga-A is really like. The rest of you have tried to forget it because she was so very sorry and because you think you're weaker than her, you think she's better at coping with adult life or whatever. Obviously, I don't agree (like, <u>at all</u>). All I can do here is hope that on some level you realise that those three weeks of Kinga-A wasn't a case of us being weaker than her, but a case of us respecting each other – and Kinga-A – more than she respects us.

I'll tell you something else for free: I'm not backing down again.

This hussy pushes herself forward as the best Kinga, the proud and gracious big sister Benek prefers. Yet Kinga-A isn't the one who made sure that Benek started out on the path he told her he wanted to be on – impersonating our mother on the phone on days when school had to be bunked, promising tickets for the premiere of Benek's first big film left right and centre in exchange for a) studio-quality portfolio photographs, b) high-resolution footage of the boy wonder reciting 'The Grave of the Countess Potocki' and c) a couple of pairs of black jeans and a couple of black turtlenecks so our brother could walk into auditions as James Dean Jr. It was Kinga-C who did all that; she got the entire village believing. She did everything that Kinga-A couldn't bring herself to do. Kinga-A only saw that Benek's path led him thousands of kilometres away from us, and she would have held on to him with a vice-like grip, cooing all the while: 'Oh, Benek, I support you, you're free to go where you're wanted, I don't mind being left behind here without any hope or even a single hobby, no, I don't mind at all, you just go ahead and cross the globe . . .'

And then the boy wouldn't have gone anywhere. Which wouldn't have been all that terrible – Benek the car mechanic would entertain himself just as well as Benek of the Moving Pictures, I reckon. He'd most likely have become a much smaller human, though, adjusting everything he did and everything he was to account for the limited amount of space within his big sister's clutches. One of my earliest memories is of watching Kinga-A clinging to Benek in that revolting way. We've got six years on the boy – there was no excuse for it . . . I moved from observer to intervener, and then there was no going back.

It wasn't Kinga-A who converted into a mnemonic machine so that our brother was word-perfect for auditions whether he liked preparing for them or not: that was me. And it definitely wasn't Kinga-A who got out of the way once she realised how much easier it'd be for everybody else if she just stayed with Babcia and Dziadek. Kinga-D, it was you who calmly waved our mother and brother off at the airport every time they went away, you're the one who held still and finished school out in the countryside, you went to see Mum and Benek wherever they happened to be, whenever you were invited, never showed envy or raised any depressing topics and never acted as if you had a right to ask them to change any of the many, many plans that meant you only saw them twice a year at most. Kingas E and F, you sent the bad boyfriends packing. And before any housefly got swatted, it was named after some industry person who was refusing to let our brother prosper in one way or another. All six of us have been better big sisters than Kinga-A has.

But I realise I have to drop it; there's only so much I can say about someone who isn't around to speak in her own defence. Mses Sikora, hear me out on this if on nothing else: yesterday's attack on Kinga-G was political. Don't get dragged into the game. St Cunigunde's day will be no different from last year, or the year before – no different from any other day, actually. But only if we don't freak out and play right into the hands of the person who'd benefit most from our feeling unsafe.

I've been writing to you and working on client profiles at the same time. The reports are suffering . . . and I've just seen that one of our new clients was born on 3 March – St Cunigunde's day! Not to be superstitious, but I think I'd better crack on with those reports now. More at lunchtime.

: :

Heading home now – I'm writing this on the metro, and it feels so wonderfully safe to do so, since none of the usual chancers want anything to do with a lady who opens a notebook on her lap and sets about scribbling with the tip of her tongue stuck out as she considers her phrasing. Now then, where was I? I was telling you about this morning. After my patriotic shower session, I got our coffee machine going (yes, the lovely bit of gear that Kinga-A ignores because it wasn't bought on discount) and headed back to the bedroom to grab our notebook, but was stopped dead in my tracks by a dejected voice from behind the pantry door asking for an encore of 'Kde domov můj'. 'Normally I wouldn't ask,' he rumbled, 'it's just . . . it would be such a comfort . . .'

I tried the door. It was locked. I found the key, and a hammer, said, 'Make yourself decent, sir – I'm coming in,' and made a slow entrance with the hammer held behind my back. The overhead light was on; he can't have got much sleep. He held his bound hands out to me and spoke with his eyelids lowered more than halfway: 'You must be Kinga-Blažena,' he said. 'I've heard a lot about you.'

I commanded myself not to shiver. Instead, I tried to get warm. Two buttons of my pyjama shirt were undone; I did them up and only felt colder.

'You're the one who says love must endure seven trials,' he said. I thought, I should speak, I can't be a silent audience for what this random captive has to say, but my tongue felt cumbersome – my whole body did, all flesh and fluids dropping below zero. I had this fear that I would freeze if he continued telling me what he'd heard. I had to speak, so I did. I said something like *Hi, how are you*. Sigh.

He shook his head. 'Not so good, Kinga-B. Remorseful over

my behaviour yesterday. If you free me, I promise I'll tell you whatever you want to know. Or I can tell you first and then you free me, but please—'

Coffee. The cup was right there in my hand. Still warm, too. I took a few sips while I looked him over. He watched my coffee consumption with a rigid set to his jaw, mostly managing to keep himself from swallowing every time I swallowed. I looked down at him, he looked up at me with something close to a shrug: 'Try, then,' he said. 'Try to place me.' As I already told you, I was the second Kinga-domino he'd toppled. He had me feeling rather womanly now that he wasn't saying anything that made me sad (I suppose that's what that freezing feeling was? It's been a while). Not just womanly, but a woman scorned. Mses Sikora, I know this man from somewhere! But I honestly can't tell you where the familiarity lies. It's not in his voice, nor in his face – well, not really. What else can it be, then – some mannerism, what? Anyway. This is someone I've been swindled by before. A minor rip-off, since I can't recall what it was I'd been manoeuvred into giving him. That's the way with gigantic cons – they start small. You have half a gram of faith in humanity left, someone asks to borrow a sliver of that, pledging to multiply it one thousandfold, and of course that sliver is gone for good. Well, he'd better have made the most of whatever he got back then, because he's not getting any more.

'What's your name again?' I asked.

'Jaroslav – ah . . . Jarda.' He looked down as soon as I made eye contact.

I put the hammer and the coffee cup on the floor, pulled

66

some scissors out of a pouch on the back of the door and went over to him.

'A knife yesterday . . . a hammer and scissors today . . .' He seemed offended, but this was most likely bravado; I was glad to note that he was shrinking back slightly, his body language telling me that the self-assurance had drained away and he'd have preferred it if I'd stayed where I was. Good good. 'What'll you threaten me with tomorrow?' he continued. 'A chainsaw?'

'Hold still, Jaroslav-ah-Jarda.' I cut his wrist ties and ankle ties and offered him coffee.

He accepted, but pointed at my cup: 'I'll finish yours, if that's OK with you.'

'That's fine,' I told him, standing in the doorway while he rotated his wrists and ankles, rose to a standing position and then flopped down again. 'Just leave once you've finished.'

'L-leave?' Instantly wary, he set his coffee cup down.

'Yes. It's not a trick, just go. I've got to go out soon, but I'll take my time getting ready, so there's no need to rush.'

'Oh,' Jarda said.

'Oh?' I said.

He drank some coffee, eyed me in an Oliver Twist sort of way – it seemed as if he was about to ask for breakfast, but instead he asked if I wanted to know how he'd ended up in the pantry.

'No, that's OK.'

Jarda opened his mouth, closed it again, scratched his chin, generally seemed at a loss as to what to say next, so I told him: 'If I was in the wrong, young man, it's safe to forgive me. This

67

won't happen again. If you were in the wrong, I'll assume you've learned a lesson about how not to behave. All's well that ends well, yes?'

'What won't happen again?' Jarda asked.

I playfully swung the hammer at him. 'This,' I said.

He didn't flinch this time, but he did raise his eyebrows before delivering a summary on my behalf: 'You don't know what happened, and you don't want to know.'

'That's right. Feel free to leave as soon as you're ready – no need to worry about saying goodbye.'

That should have been that. Kinga-B finds someone broken yet alluring in our pantry, sends him out for repairs, the crisis is averted, and both our weeks are saved – his and mine. But no. Jarda knocked on my bedroom door just as I'd finished skim-reading yesterday's diary entry with urgent reference to the passages concerning him. I was already dressed for work, so I told him to come in.

'No, you come out, please,' he said, firmly.

He walked ahead of me to the sitting room, sat down on the sofa and patted the space beside him: 'We have to talk.'

Why was he making it so hard for me to do the right thing? 'You seem reluctant to get out of here, Jaroslav-ah-Jarda. Did something change overnight? After all, you were trying to get Siri to call the police yesterday.'

Siri clinked into action: *Hi Kinga, did you just ask me to call the police?*

'NO—' Jarda and I shouted as one.

Then, to me, he said: 'She told you I tried to escape?'

68

She . . .

'Clearly recollections of yesterday vary,' I said. 'That's all over, though. Today you're a free agent. I'm sure people are worried about you, probably searching for you as we speak—'

Jarda stopped me there: 'No, I've used up a week of my holiday allowance at work, and anyone who might have got worried already knows not to get in contact for a while.'

'OK, well, you can hide out somewhere else – do you understand me?'

He pouted, I warned myself I could not, should not and must not resort to the 'go on, shoo' one says to a stubborn kitten or puppy, and lo, another possibility occurred to me.

'Are you waiting for me to return something of yours? Am I meant to give you lunch money?'

He pulled his phone out of one pocket, a credit card and some folding money out of another pocket and waved both handfuls of valuables at me. The phone was switched off. I started to get interested in that, then shut the interest off pronto.

'Listen,' Jarda said. 'I'm in a sticky situation here. The stickiest yet. And I made a bad start with Kinga-Alojzia – it must have been the stress. I totally misjudged the right approach to take with her. Kinga-Filoména did say I should just tell her the truth, but at the last minute I thought it'd be better to, well, you know, flirt a little bit. When that flopped, I had another bad idea, and by then there was nothing I could say. But I'm playing it straight now.'

I'd made up my mind to greet that outpouring with a sneer,

but his flirtation concept – inviting his target to stab him – pulled up one corner of my mouth and then the other. He started smiling back, and snowballs and ice cubes started piling up around me again. All he was doing was speaking to me, or looking at me as if he thought I was pretty; it made no sense for any of that to pierce me the way it did. It could be something to do with feeling like some sort of hag beside him. Benek's six years our junior, and this guy is quite a lot younger than Benek. Yes, maybe that's it. I feel mocked by his attention, comparing each pause and each glance with the one just before it, and there's no deciding whether this sensation of ridicule is accidental or a deliberate. Speak, I said to myself, speak.

'You're a friend of Kinga-F's?'

'I am.'

'A friend she's never mentioned.'

'I'm not surprised . . . I feel like I only hear from her when everybody else she thought of has other plans. Which is fine; being first choice puts a guy under pressure . . .'

'If you say so, Jarda.'

'I'm just a last choice of hers who's never done anything anecdote-worthy until – well, I hatched this plan. And I've been promised that you guys would help me out. Come on. Please. It's only until Sunday.'

I gave him fifteen minutes to spill the beans; no way was I going to be late in to the office because of him.

Here's the yarn our guest spun me: he's just a blameless babe who's thrown us right into the middle of Luxury Enamel Posse infighting at its most savage. It's a tale of two bosses (Ms

Cheque and Mr Calcium) in a realm where there can only be one. Jarda is Mr Calcium's son. Why is Mr Calcium called Mr Calcium? Because he provides the teeth that the Luxury Enamel Posse inundates its victims with. Ms Cheque does the cheques. But about those teeth . . . where *do* they come from? Jarda tells me 'it's no secret' that you find tons and tons of teeth wherever meteorites have struck the earth. Not actually in the impact craters, but close enough for a link to make sense. You dig until your shovel strikes the first layer of these remarkably humanoid teeth, and then you can gather a truckload's worth and keep going back for more without ever running out. No other bones, only teeth. Mr Calcium gets his from a couple of spots in the Beskid Mountains; that's the full extent of the info Jarda has on the teeth.

'OK, one more thing, Jarda . . .'

'What?'

'This Luxury Enamel Posse and their harassment of civilians – what's that about?'

He stared at me. 'What do you think it's about?'

'It's a bamboozler, Jarda. That's why I'm asking you.'

'Kinga-Blažena . . .' He tapped the side of his head: 'Wise up . . . wise up. There's money in it. Reducing property value on some streets and raising the value of properties for sale on other streets – that's how they rake it in.'

To resume Jaroslav's yarn, for the past six months or so a few close members of Mr Calcium's circle have been making unauthorised forays across the border with Slovakia. Ignorant of the true lie of the land over there, the faction led by Jaroslav's

dad paid a late-night visit to a farmstead family – dairy farm-
ers – and left them stuffed inside their own pasteurisation vats
along with the trademark blank cheques and teeth. They'd
done their research before they struck, but only in terms of
real-estate figures. It was Mr Calcium's great misfortune to
have manhandled the head of that farmstead family, who just
happens to be Ms Cheque's daughter.

'We didn't even know she had a daughter,' Jarda said. 'Let
alone a daughter across the border . . .'

Now Ms Cheque is seeking an eye for an eye. She's put out
word that Mr Calcium's son is to be brought to her immediately. There's no point protesting that Jaroslav wasn't involved,
that he wasn't there that night, that he has alibis . . . Ms Cheque
doesn't want to hear it. Now Jaroslav is having to be very careful who he talks to, where he's seen and what he says when
anybody casually asks him where he is. Everybody could be
indebted to Ms Cheque in one way or another.

I suggested that he toughen up and undergo the suitcase
treatment, and he said 'Fuck that! Why should I?'

'Well, Jarda . . . why should anybody have to go through
that sort of thing? And yet they have. In your case, you might
consider it a form of tax on a cushy life.'

'I don't have a cushy life. I've done everything by the book,
same as you, Kinga-B. And I'm claustrophobic. I almost die
even just thinking about being zipped up in a suitcase.'

'So the plan you hatched was . . . ?'

'To pre-empt Ms Cheque. I vanish for a little while, Kinga-F
sends photos of me looking very much the worse for wear

to this blowhard I know, the blowhard passes them on to Ms Cheque, maybe also taking responsibility for giving Ms Cheque the revenge she wanted, and the whole situation blows over.'

Even if a single word of this is true, Jarda must think Ms Cheque is a moron.

Oh, and Kinga-F? If Jarda told you this and you said 'Count me in', you're a moron too.

I pushed him out of the front door ahead of me. He dug his heels in, making all kinds of declarations regarding the blood I'll have on my hands. Whenever we reached complete stand-still, I tickled him so that he ran forward – I don't think it was a guess, I think I knew that this man can't abide being tickled. I think that's when I seriously began to worry that he could be a variable that wrests next Tuesday out of my control. Not just next Tuesday – maybe all of the Tuesdays.

.. ..

Mses Sikora, yr story time host got home to find an extensive-ly hooded figure sitting cross-legged beside our front door. The hood flopped down so far over his face that all I saw were golden eyes looking out of the shadows. The floral-print res-pirator mask lightened the tone a little, but only a very little. I thought – well, throwing himself upon his mark's mercy hasn't worked, so now he's going to force his way in. I'd only just got off the phone; I'd been telling Dr Holý that his call with Kinga-A had been a storm in a teacup, and he didn't seem to know what I was referring to . . . that could've just been him being discreet, but he's also a funny one in his own way, our doctor . . .

Better to turn to the Law.

'Hey, Siri,' I said.

'Not so fast, not so fast,' he said, holding up a paper bag. A Wolt delivery.

I asked what was in the bag, and he showed me. Two portions of miso soup and two blossom- and seed-strewn avocados.

'Kinga-B,' he said, 'I really can't leave the building – it's too risky. But, for you, I figured out a way to order this without switching on my phone. I'm not trying to buy myself an invitation to dinner – to be honest I could have both soups and both avocados and still not feel as if I'd even had a snack. I'm just trying to show you I'm not here to take anything from you.'

'Alright,' I said, taking the paper bag, opening the front door and pointing the way with my chin. 'Get in.'

I don't have a bucket list. If this is my last Tuesday evening, I'm alright with having spent it drinking Mattoni, nibbling on greenery and . . . how to describe the rest? I brought our fluffiest blankets out, started up my '101 Renditions of Mack the Knife' playlist, and we got cosy – or at least, I did. Jarda wound a blanket around himself but sat at my feet, answering my questions with an unblushing bravado that I recognise from my exam-taking, academic-assignment-completing days: *Well, here's what I found in my head. See – there are a few things in there . . . just not the things you've asked about.*

'You seem confident,' I said to him, wanting to see if he liked the sound of that. He didn't.

He crossed and uncrossed his arms, sort of smiled – well, it looked more like a bitter lip-twist, really.

'Confident,' he said. 'Really. Would you be, if you were me?'

'Probably. As you, I'd probably be thinking, OK, there may be seven of them, but since there's shared hardware, there are bound to be reliable links between their thought processes. I just have to test a few principles on one of them and, if my hypotheses are proven, that's my lodgings for the week sorted, since I'll already have the other six in the palm of my hand.'

'My gut's already warning me that's not the way to, ah, harmony,' he said, having abandoned his attempts to smile. 'Harmonious coexistence for five more days, that's all I have in mind. But just out of interest, could you help me out with a reason why the approach you mentioned would fail?'

'There's bound to be one . . . at least one of us, who isn't going to care about you or your life precisely because the others seem to place some value on both.'

He nodded. 'Yeah, I've been thinking about how to handle that. You're warning me about one, but I'm anticipating two or more. Pretending that the rest of you dislike me is—'

'Completely see-through. You can forget that right now.'

'No matter how heartless or ignoble those Kingas are, they're still only human, right? So there'll be a way to appeal to them. And I'll find it somehow. I have to.'

'What? You can't expect me to believe you'd show up unprepared.'

Jarda shrugged. 'Neither can I, Kinga-B . . . neither can I. Yet here we are.'

I pummelled him with scepticism and barely left a dent; it was as if he was holding his ground from behind a giant punch shield. And his resistance was more comforting than any embrace could have been. An example: this job he's taken a week off from – he claims to be a bailiff. And his bailiff tales make his explanation about the Luxury Enamel Posse's tooth supply sound mundane.

'How well do you know the Bohnice area?' I asked him, for want of a more subtle way of asking him if he's ever been a psychiatric patient who might have accompanied a lookalike of mine on Sunday walks amongst budding magnolias.

He rubbed his chin. 'Bohnice?' For a moment – less than a moment – he was at a loss, then those lion eyes lit up. 'Kinga, you've seen pictures of the Terracotta Army, right?'

I have. Having been buried with thousands of terracotta soldiers to guard him in the afterlife, the first emperor of China – the first ruler who proved capable of unifying that immense (and immensely complex) mesh of kingdoms – is as exceptional in death as he was in life. We talked about the other terracotta figures that had been discovered near the tomb . . . close to a whole society of figurines.

'Well, picture a similar set-up,' Jarda said, 'Only on a smaller scale due to budget constraints . . . and in a vault beneath Bohnice Cemetery,' Jarda said.

It had all begun in Smíchov in 1985. The pre-eminent Smíchov watering hole at that time had a workaholic landlord who keeled over behind the bar one night. All his regulars felt the loss, but also felt this was the exit he'd have chosen. Everybody attended the funeral, after which the landlord's body was removed to his family vault in Bohnice. The funeral guests repaired to the pub to raise a glass to the dead man, but an appalling scene ensued. The dead landlord – or, rather, his ghoul – greeted the mourners from behind the bar, declaring that there'd be no free drinks today, it was business as usual. Regulars screamed, regulars fainted, priests were brought in, but the landlord wouldn't budge. No heaven, hell, reincarnation or oblivion for him: he was staying in the place where master brewers had perfected the art, the place where the earth's saltiest drank their daily bread. A one-sided commitment: his pub became a no-go area – as did the surrounding neighbourhood. Something about a ghostly landlord just makes you think too much and puts you off your beer. Eventually the landlord's heirs found a solution: expanding the family vault so that it included a facsimile pub where the landlord could cater to terracotta regulars until he got tired of it. The landlord thought it over and it didn't seem any lonelier than the way things were with real live regulars staying away, so . . .

'Jarda,' I said, 'If you want to tell me that you evicted a landlord's ghost for being behind with family vault payments . . .'

'No, no, it was the squatters who had to go. One hundred per cent land-of-the-living stuff. They'd heard that story about the creation of the Terracotta Pub, but they were fearless. That's all you need to rob the dead – brass balls. These unauthorised tenants . . . oh, sorry, just a minute – I think the past couple of days are catching up with me . . . *hnfffff.* Jarda's slump was so sudden; fatigue darted in and dealt him a knockout blow. His eyes fluttered shut and his chin sank chestwards. I finally switched off the song of pearly teeth and fancy gloves and I fetched pillows, thinking, *Alright, you're earning your keep.*

He's asleep on the sofa now, and I've begun dozing a little myself. Goodnight.

WEDNESDAY

Friends! Poppies! Countrywomen! I ignored my soothing birdsong alarm this morning, but the curtains were open, so the sky tossed bucketfuls of tinsel on my head until there was simply no staying under the covers any more. You'll doubtless be annoyed to read that I may even have emerged grinning. It can't be helped when you think what a sunny, rainy morning like this means: multicoloured bridges between the clouds by afternoon. As if that weren't enough to put a girl in a good mood, I was served breakfast in bed. Your Kinga-Casimira is grateful to whichever of you brought this DISH to our yard. I'm not so sure about his looks. Didn't realise this is the kind of physique you go for, poppies . . . glossy-magazine rugged? It's good to be handsome and all that, but all things in moderation, if you please. A scar or facial birth mark, a wonkier nose, larger ears – any two out of those three, or some other factor you could see he's had to work around, and he'd be *perfect*. No, it's his helpfulness and politeness that bring him up to at least a nine. His girlfriend hasn't done too badly for herself.

Juicy J (who says this is the second-worst nickname that's ever been forced on him) knocked on our door with a <u>scrupulously</u> prepared tray just as I'd begun catching up with our chronicle. I was all 'Pleased to meet you, I'm Kinga-Casimira, and you are . . . ?'

He surveyed the room pretty thoroughly as he introduced

himself, and I noticed him noticing the rollerball pen in my hand. Well, I thought it was the pen that was surprising him until he said: 'You're left-handed.'

For some reason he seemed rather spooked by that – I mean, on the verge of running out of the room spooked. Hmmmm. Not only is he acquainted with one of you right-handed poppies, but you've written things down – whole diary entries, perhaps – in his presence. I put the pen down, and he got apologetic: 'I shouldn't have said that out loud.'

'Story of my life,' I said, digging into breakfast (I'd only dropped the pen to pick up cutlery). 'Let's not be nervous around each other . . . any friend of Kinga-B's is a friend of mine. Will you be staying long?'

'Only until Sunday,' he said, not yet at ease but gradually getting there, 'then I'll be out of your hair.'

Good thing I was scheduled for a late start today. Not being a bookworm, I get diary-reading out of the way first thing. If I didn't do that, I wouldn't hear from any of you ever. Some of you have probably guessed this, but I'm hereby bringing my laziness out into the open: when I have to go in early, I take a look at Tuesday's entry, and leave things there. What? On an ordinary week, a summary of Tuesday is all I need. That paragraph or so lets me know I'm starting with a reasonably clean slate, what with our most esteemed Kinga-B having hacked any roadblocks to pieces. I can throw on my leather jacket and sally forth a free woman . . .

Today, after reading Kinga-B's entry I actually had to go back and read Kinga-A's. Then, for the first time in months, I read about Sunday, Saturday, Friday and Thursday as well – in that order. Each of those entries consisted of four or five lines, and everybody was saying more or less what I'd expected them to say. It was all so quiet before Monday, wasn't it? All of us keeping things back, sweeping the mess away into the margins because our arrangement simply has to work. We've already split the weeks, months and years ahead of us into the most manageable pieces possible, all we have to do now is trust each other. I try to imagine Kinga-A pushing us all out of the way and taking it all on, Kinga-A alone on that harmony-and-approval-seeking grind every day, and, yeah, I don't see it, my poppies. Even I can see that she has a tendency to butter us up, but that's obviously guilt-driven. Kinga-Blažena, you think we do more for our leader than she does for us, and our leader agrees. Why not shake hands on that and cool down? You're both wrong, but that's a minor detail.

About the fight during quarantine with Benek: I hadn't realised things were that bad between you two. I'm not sure what I would have said or done if Kinga-A had come to me and (hopefully) made her case for taking the whole three weeks – I'd probably have said fine, or tried to swing an agreement that let me have Mondays AND Wednesdays for three weeks, that sort of thing. But I had no contact with her or with any of you. From where I'm sitting, the most alarming part of those lost weeks was that every Wednesday I thought I had woken up and had a normal Wednesday. Normal for me, that is, though I do remember feeling relief that the trip to France had been called off. I slipped into those day-long hallucinations so seamlessly, and while they were ongoing, I didn't suspect a thing and happily ran, jumped, swung across and climbed mirages, lay in the arms of spectres, a phantasm among phantasms, basically. I still don't understand how I went missing like that. It's true that I really didn't want to spend my precious Wednesday in close quarters with Benek . . .

Don't get me wrong, it's so nice that you poppies are fond of the guy. I just don't really have any feelings left when it comes to him. Must've overdosed on Benek-related emotions when we were young. All that hype-woman activity Kinga-B talked about – that could've been the burn-out factor. For me the holiday in France was like, great, I've got to spend three Wednesdays in a row with the Boy Wonder. I knew I wasn't going to be able to hide my 'meh'. But I also didn't want to rock the boat by trying to get out of it . . . three Wednesdays is better than three whole weeks, right? Then, somehow, I excused myself from even the 'three Wednesdays' obligation. I'd be pleased if I knew how I did it, or if I was certain that the disappearance was under my control? However: Kinga-B, whilst overpowering you, our leader outright neglected me. That's what I was raging about. Her just taking over my day without trying to find out where I'd gone. She did write that she was worried but didn't want to interfere with my independence, though. And since I actually was OK there isn't anything else to whinge about.

To be absolutely clear, I won't be joining you on strike, Kinga-B. And I'm not siding with you either, Kinga-A. I'm just over here trying not to get shakshuka on these pages while I write. Shakshuka cooked right in our kitchen. It was so good I had to check on the chef's marital status: 'Mmmph, I could kiss you! But your significant other would most likely hate that . . .'

'Yes, she would,' he said gravely. 'And so would yours. Well, enjoy . . .'

'Hold on – where are you going? You can't just run off like that without telling me how you know about my significant other. Take a seat. No, not over there. There's really no need to be so shy – you're perfectly safe here.'

Juicy J patted the bedcovers to ascertain the location of my legs and settled down on an unoccupied sector of the mattress. 'I'm not shy,' he said. With a murmured 'May I?' he reached over my tray and poured a little more oat milk into my cup of Earl Grey, securing that effect of smooth roasted petals stirred into zingy dew. 'That was just a guess about you being with someone. Tell me something about your relationship and I'll tell you something about mine?'

'Deal,' I said, passing him a couple of cushions. 'Well, for starters, we're long-distance.'

'Really,' he said. 'How long-distance?'

'Well, he lives in Prague 10, so it's really hard for us. No . . . I mean, I wish that was the type of obstacle we had to over-come! The distance isn't between places. It's a time thing.'

I told Juicy J all about it. Don't bother lecturing me about oversharing; he did ask. Just let me talk about my doomed love! I won't let you treat him as a grubby memory. The long-distance element of this relationship is the realisation, unfolded across decades of meeting all sorts of other people, that nobody is as interesting to me as that boy. The time we spent together was hardly a meeting of minds – or anything else – it was more or less babysitting. Yet those few weeks have become the reason I avoid romantic ties. My rationale: this way, if and when that boy appears before me as a man, there won't be any obstacles on my side – I won't have to undo any second-, third- or fourth-best bonds, I can just go straight to him. After removing all and any obstacles on his side, of course.

'Oh yeah? What made that kid such a big deal to you?' Juicy J asked.

Something, just something. Or maybe it was all a delusion of mine and he was just some boy who kept coming over to Babcia and Dziadek's house to join the queue of other boys requesting Benek's participation in their outdoor games. The other boys asked in a spirit of optimism, seeing no reason why access to Benek would be denied, whereas when this boy said 'Can Benek please come out to play?' he baulked at the sound of his own speech. It was as if he was asking for the moon and knew there was no logical reason why he should ever be granted such largesse, yet he couldn't not ask. It's the way of the world that Benek was all but oblivious to his first fan, and for some reason I decided that this time it wouldn't do. This time I was going to work a miracle. Or maybe I just wanted to be treated to the sight of an unlikely friendship – it's hard to know why one does things. Whatever the reason, this boy was going to get what he lacked and what he needed: my brother's fellowship, a kind word or two, a warm glance that he could probably eke out for another thirty or forty weeks, etc. And in the end Benek did ask that boy to go along on group bike rides a couple of times.

Juicy J said he wanted to know how Benek was persuaded to do that.

'I went to him and I said "Listen carefully, Benek, this is a boy you're meant to be friends with. He's been sent to you by David Hasselhoff."'

'David . . . Hasselhoff? From *Baywatch*?'

'The very same. Benek worshipped him. Still does. Saying "David Hasselhoff would approve" was a pretty reliable way of getting him to do something. Especially if you hadn't tried to influence his behaviour for six months or so. But if you tried to ban something by telling him David Hasselhoff *wouldn't* approve, Benek would titter piously and tell you that the Hoff forgives. He had a poster of David Hasselhoff as the Knight Rider, and he'd chatter away at it, trying to get a conversation going with David. All in vain, since the poster only communicated with me. I was able to pronounce a handful of words that sounded kind of American to a clueless eight-year-old, you see . . .'

'Ah, so Benek let this boy tag along until you were exposed as a false prophet.'

'Something like that, yeah.'

I think what it truly came down to was the contrast between this would-be friend and his other playmates. They didn't have much spite in them, those boys, they were raucous moppets who got on best with equally mouthy kids they could push over and get knocked down by without setting some sort of parental tribunal in motion. Konrad – that was this boy's name – couldn't really operate in an environment of casual aggression. You looked at the way he was dressed, you noticed the way he walked and talked; it was easy to imagine getting in big trouble if this kid so much as caught a cold in your vicinity. Konrad had spent most of his life at an orphanage – that's how he and Benek met; our school regularly sent its pupils on trips to national landmarks in the same coach as the orphanage kids. Message: misfortune only divides us if we let it. Benek charmed Konrad somehow; there could've been a memorable lunchbox item swap, something like that. It's easy to get caught off guard by my brother's attitude as he gives his favourite things away – he usually seems relieved. Intriguing as Konrad might have found this, good news removed him from our village scene – he got adopted by a wealthy couple who lived in Krakow. It seemed safe to assume we'd seen the last of him until he knocked on Babcia's door, looking as if he'd walked (or more likely tumbled) all the way across the country. He asked if Benek was at home. Yes, my brother was at home, until he resigned himself to committing another sin that David Hasselhoff was just going to have to forgive. He went out with the fun crowd and left strict injunctions not to tell Konrad where he could be found. *If Konrad keeps trying to hang around with us,* Benek warned, *I'll make a FRIGHTFUL scene.*

Juicy J was lying on his front, listening with his chin resting on both hands. Every now and then he raised a calf in the air and twirled his ankle. When I looked at him, he said: 'Did you hate being the much less sought-after sibling?'

'Who says I was much less sought after?'

'You're the one saying it. Periphrastically.'

'Peri what?'

'In a roundabout way. Yet the painfulness is plain.'

'Nonsense. There wasn't any pain.'

'No? So where does Konrad come into this? You were hospitable to him so he wouldn't have had a wasted journey, and . . . ?'

'Oh. Right. I'd sort out Konrad's snack time, we jumped in rain puddles and played board games, but sometimes, when I couldn't think of anything else to keep him busy, I'd tell him to close his eyes and I'd say "watch out, watch out, Konrad, watch out", and then I'd blow bubbles at him. He'd keep his eyes closed, and it must've felt good when they struck his skin and burst, because he'd laugh and laugh. Pretty unforgettable, let me tell you – that kid clothed in all those flashing spheres he couldn't see, and when he laughed, they broke open. And then, ugh, he'd say *Thank you, Kinga!*'

Juicy J gave me an 'awww', and asked what Konrad looked like.

'A bear cub. He was hairy and he lumbered around.'

'Clumsy?'

'Not at all. It was like he was controlling or directing some bulk only he was aware of, so it was up to him not to wreck other people's stuff. His expressions changed really slowly too. He checked your expression before crafting his. I think that's because he was smiley by nature. I heard he kept getting told off at the orphanage for seeming cheerful when he wasn't meant to be.'

'So your ideal partner is the one who's willing to get excited about nothing, or however that commandment of Warhol's goes . . . ?'

'That's only half of the ideal. The other half is getting terribly, terribly sad when given something to weep about. I'd alternate between *watch out, watch out*, and bubbles and telling Konrad bubbles were on the way, then flicking his forehead really hard. And then all was woe! His *owww* would've broken a heart even harder than mine. Sometimes he'd apologise without explaining what for. He could've been thinking that if he volunteered to take the blame we'd be back to bubbles again? Anyway, that was up to an hour's entertainment. Watch out, watch out and a forehead flick, or here come the bubbles followed by bubbles, or watch out, watch out and then lots and lots of bubbles twice in a row with watch out, watch out and a forehead flick immediately afterwards, and that boy Konrad just kind of cascaded between *owww* and *thank you*, apparently without predicting or fearing or hoping for the next choice I would make. I never understood why he didn't get angry and shout *stop it*, or threaten to tell on me unless I stuck with bubbles only. He was just . . .'

'What an odd child,' said Juicy J.

'Oh, yes.'

'Did it ever cross your mind that he might develop some weird ideas about girls because of you?'

'Oh, no. I wasn't anything remotely resembling a girl to him. That's probably the reason we were able to make do with each other's company.'

'Oh. Well, you've had more time to mull the whole thing over, so I'll take your word for it. I do want to say this, though – why not drop this ideal while you still can? Strange kids are strangely good at dispensing disappointment. We could even call it their speciality. Every single baby oddball I ever kept track of grew up into some kind of conformist. Sometimes to an overbearing extent.'

'Haha. Don't worry, the disappointment's already been dispensed.'

'How? By failing to show up in adult form?'

'No, it was later the same year.'

Juicy J asked what had happened. I'd have been happy to fill him in, but I don't remember. I only remember reeling the way you do after a smack to the head – that sensation of sinuses scraped so hollow that when you breathe in the air whirls around screeching between skull and skin. An overreaction, of course. Just as the entire Konrad fascination is, if you ask Dr Holý. (Our dear doctor doesn't put it as bluntly as that, but I see what he's getting at with his musings as to whether I've ever actually met a boy that I find interesting or whether it tends to be a case of me talking myself into finding them interesting.)

'Did you ever ask Kinga-Blažena about your Konrad?'

'No. Why would I?'

'You have that option. I think she remembers the particulars.'

Kinga-B remembering things I don't, keeping them from me but blabbing to Juicy J . . . ? That can't be true. Juicy J and his lies. It seems like he just can't help himself. I didn't comment, I only reminded him of our deal. 'So, I told you about mine. Time to talk about yours.'

'You're going to think I'm copying you,' he said, 'but mine's long-distance too.'

'Across time as well?'

He said it wasn't that, and it wasn't place-related either. Here's the sum total of what Juicy J divulged re: his main squeeze: 'She's my best friend. No, that sounds – ugh, what I mean is, she's the person I know best. And she knows me. Really knows, you know? She's also . . . hmmm, exactly my kind of alluring. The very epitome of "come hither". So I'm trying to go thither. She has some overprotective siblings that want placating, but . . . yeah. We'll see, I guess.'

That's what he said, and this is what I heard: *We're going through a rough patch. She's probably about to leave me even though I'm hanging on to her for dear life.*

Juicy J didn't want to confide in me, and that's his prerogative, though a tad insulting given that he was so chatty with you, Kinga-A and Kinga-B, linking himself to real-estate bandits and whatnot. Where's that boldness now? Broadening the scope of my grievance, didn't swains used to be much more eloquent when it came to their lady loves? Is my own bestie, Berenika, right to contend that there never was a time like that, it was just poets with big shirt collars taking the piss out of us all . . . a rose-coloured-lens cartel whose depravity is only rivalled by the likes of the Luxury Enamel Posse? Answers on a postcard, if you please, poppies.

'Have you eaten?' I asked.

He told me he had.

'Don't you need some fresh air? You can come to work with me, if you want.'

'I can?' He was not indifferent to that offer, but stuck to his thing about needing to stay out of sight.

My breakfast was getting cold, so I demolished it once and for all. 'This shakshuka! What did you do to make it so good?'

He beamed. 'It's great to see you enjoying it. I was on auto-pilot . . .'

He unwound enough to reminisce about working at The Hummus Bar, where the shakshuka has to be up to Tel Aviv standards. And he offered a second breakfast if I was up to it: the best porridge in the city. He learned to make that at The Oat Bar. He's worked at other places across the city too. Not only food places; Juicy J's got quite a few under his belt. He says, with only the tiniest twitch of irony, that when he was younger, he used to be told he'd go far.

I didn't have room for porridge, and I really did have to get going, but I felt bad about leaving him on his own indoors all day. I was picturing him wistfully watching the rainbow from the window and so on. But he says he doesn't miss using his phone, since he mainly uses it for strident phone calls, strongly worded e-mails and depositing flame emojis and comments like PIMPIN' PIMPIN' beneath his friends' social-media posts. He's looking forward to getting some reading done today. Oh, and he gave me a roll of camera film I'm dropping off at my mate Tonda's place on the way to work. Snapshots of a forlorn and zip-tied coder/bailiff/line cook/car mechanic (et al.) are pure muesli in comparison to some of the other photos I've glimpsed in Tonda's darkroom. I think it would've been good to take some more in case Kinga-F missed any convincing angles, but Juicy J says it was a fairly thorough photoshoot . . .

The customary long-ish search for my unicorn wellies was halved today; I had Juicy J rummaging along with me! I don't doubt that there'll come a day when I'm forced to conclude that one of you has made good on your threats to get rid of my rain boots. For now . . . 'thanks' for letting them stay another week. I sat down to pull the wellies on, and when I stood up and reached for my trench coat, it wasn't there. Juicy J had already taken it off the rack. He helped me into my coat, left arm, right arm, the warmth of his touch passing from my shoulder to my wrist, where he tugged the sleeves so they covered the cuffs of my jumper. It felt good to let him do that. I liked what I was seeing, too, this big man dressing a doll with the tender solemnity that separates doll stylists from measly dilettantes. Once it was over, I thanked him and headed for the door, waving goodbye. 'Going out into the rain like this,' he said, planting himself in my path, 'is like putting yourself on a fast track to catching a cold. May I finish?'

'Oh,' I said. 'Go on, then – but make it snappy.'

Poppies, I've made quite some noise about our guest not being to my personal taste – I know I have. But that was before he served an appetiser. He did up my coat buttons, looped the belt around my waist and drew me two, then three steps towards him as he tied his knot, not looking at me, his eyes on the curve he was emphasising with his hands. And how that emphasis of his made itself felt; it was like smoke pouring down my navel and nestling between my thighs. Juicy J went on chiding me with a look that was both stern and wicked, he was telling me that it may look chic to run around in the rain with a coat flapping all over the place, but keeping warm is better. I agreed. I agreed very quietly, with my fingers trailing through his hair. Two can perform grooming rituals . . . that was all I meant to demonstrate. I played with his earring and had myself a bit of a smirk, but the joke turned out to be on me – a gentle(ish) greed set in. I spiralled his thick, dark locks around my fingertips and pulled just a little, spreading my hand until I was cupping his neck. He tried and failed to catch his breath, and that was delicious. Even more delicious: with his eyes on me instead of on the trench coat now, he turned his head so that his lips brushed my thumb as he spoke: 'What are you doing, Kinga-Casimira?'

'Nothing. What are *you* doing?'

Apparently, that was all it took to restore Juicy J to his better judgement. He studied my belted waist again, and, finally content with the result, he unhanded me. No, he did a bit more than that. He grabbed my umbrella, walked me downstairs and, leaning out of the main door of the building, he opened the umbrella so I could step out under it.

'Not coming with me, then?' I asked.

'Even if I could, I'm not your type, remember? Off you go, minx.'

::

I keep looking at one particular exchange of messages on our phone. It's from Monday, so from Kinga-A, to a contact saved as 'Milica'.

> Kinga-A: Milica, I have to ask . . . why did you say I'm a talented masseuse?
>
> Milica: Well, you might be. You don't know for sure that you aren't!
>
> Kinga-A: ?
>
> Milica: You might be a masseuse on another day of the week!
>
> Kinga-A: Not sure what you're getting at, but I'd appreciate it if you could stick to known facts (very few of which are available on both sides at this point in time!)
>
> Milica: Not sure why the thought of having healing hands bothers you so much, but fine.

So, you know the 'she's out to get us' feeling that Kinga-A has when she reflects on Kinga-G's Sunday subterfuge (which, by the way, is more of a prank than anything else, surely)? The same feeling that Kinga-B has about Kinga-A? That's what I'm getting from Milica.

::

Just left Tonda's place; these days he's got a couple of antique rocking horses set up in his living room, so naturally we had to ride those things competitive jockey style until one of us won the race – we couldn't decide who, but we kind of had the time of our lives, so . . .

I just re-read that, and I want to make sure any euphemism-hunters amongst you understand that I'm speaking literally, about actual rocking horses. Fumigate your minds, please!

I'll have to trouble you to pick Juicy J's photos up on Friday, Kinga-Eliška. I already gave Tonda his photo-developing fee: Berenika's most frequently used phone number. Much good may that do him . . .

::

Now I'm in the staff changing rooms at the hotel just off Václavák. I just got into my window-cleaning gear and we're waiting for our only latecomer so the crew leader won't have to keep sending our platforms up and down like some kind of taxi service. I'll put this notebook in a locker when Vincenzo gets here – otherwise I can see it getting left behind in one of these bags and belts I'm loaded up with. Sponges, scrapers, spray bottles, brushes; most of the other hotel crew members are sitting down with all these items hanging off them. I just heard one of them say: 'NOTHING can stop me from relax-ing.' Ordinarily I'd be like that too, but today I prefer to lean against this wall so it's easier to write to you, deposit our note-book and then walk into the lift straight after. A nice man has volunteered his back as my standing desk; what more could I ask for?

Having said that, I'd adore a text message from Berenika right about now. She hasn't replied to my message letting her know that we're running late. Probably busy with honey-trap things. Our company 'goes the extra mile and then some', just as the endorsement from one of our repeat customers says. *These guys are so much more than just adventure-holiday plan-ners!* Damn right; our team of four crafts crises with care. Everyone who comes to us needs to prove that they're capa-ble of saving themselves and others. In some cases, once is enough, but there are those who think their successful hero-ism might have been a fluke, so they want to try it again with different variables, and they want us to make it more difficult than last time.

Extending protection to someone weaker usually boosts the experience of defeating the bad guys, but for that to work, the experience has to begin before our customer realises it's begun. We put our heads together, scripted the venture with flow charts addressing most eventualities, and assigned roles until there were only two left – the honey trap and the window cleaner/flea marketeer. The honey-trap role being an over-nighter, I couldn't do that one – though I'd like to while I've still got the goods. Ah well!

Yesterday evening, while Kinga-B and Juicy J were hav-ing their ascetic gala, our client, Blaise P, completed check-in at this very hotel. An establishment that just happens to be owned by my colleague Justýna's cousin. Blaise might know this, he might not – it depends on how intensive his Google searches are. Yesterday evening he would've become aware of a stunning (and distraught, but mostly stunning) personal assistant at the neighbouring check-in desk and, having offered this 'Karla' a shoulder to cry on, he would've gone from helping her search for a papier mâché 'World's Best Mum' trophy her boss's daughter had made to offering his grateful new friend a nightcap in his suite. That's the most delicate part. There are a couple of other ways we could obtain the personal effects we need to make the next stage particularly startling for our client, but Berenika's chosen to spend the night pilfering and then take the last couple of items as she leaves with him in the morning. I was slightly more in favour of Berenika and Blaise wistfully parting ways until the next coincidence. In the morning I'd have entered his room as a cleaner and cleared off with his Rolex and whatnot. Berenika nixed that; she doesn't want Blaise to get any distance from the idea of having been thrown into some sort of alliance with someone in this city. She said we should just leave this to her. It's Berenika, so no worries there, but Justýna, Vincenzo and I still tried to assist with details that might make Blaise more likely to want to celebrate finding the trophy: super-angry phone calls from the boss demanding progress reports, plus we planted two other 'World's Best Mum' trophies in the hotel lobby. Neither are the trophy Berenika's looking for, but both are meant to be discovered during the course of Blaise and Berenika's search. Kids and their way of identifying their parents' most paralysing insecurities and then pressing down hard, eh? Blaise P, more than content with Exciting Uncle status, will be able to hypothesise the reasons Berenika's boss is on a mad one over this papier mâché trophy, and he'll feel relief that he's able to participate in this search with suspended judgement. We planned that once Berenika had the correct 'World's Best Mum' trophy in hand, she'd have a moment of clarity, ring up her boss and tell her *Sorry, I think I'm going to go crazy if I keep working for you, I have to resign.* We (our company, Závin, I mean) have identified unemployment as Blaise P's greatest fear. Blaise is around the same age as us, poppies. We still have another twenty years or so left before we can go on a perpetual gallivant with spa breaks for Kinga-D, but Blaise could've already retired ten years ago if he wanted. He fears the absence of a coherent job title more than he fears military conscription, serious illness and bereavement. Blaise will have been by Berenika's side as she took her leap into the unknown – presumably that's how he'll have viewed it – and if he wasn't galvanised by that, he's on the wrong holiday.

Blaise was a teenager in the 1990s; vague memories of headlines led him to ask for some Cold War flavouring to be added to his time in Prague. Now we're giving him a quadruple pump of spy syrup that hopefully makes up for booking an adventure honeymoon and ending up doing this solo. We were lounging around on beanbags and listening on loudspeaker as Justýna talked this man out of cancelling his booking. 'Just come over, surprise yourself, save the day,' she told him. 'By day three you'll be like . . . Charlotte WHO?' Whenever Justýna needs to make difficult things sound exciting, she channels her Oregonian mother, and it works. Blaise's going to infiltrate one of those pesky blackmailing rings that has western democracy in a chokehold, forcing elected officials to do what they want 'or else' . . . from there he can go with counter-blackmail, discrediting their sources with one blow or unadulterated anarchy, but he'll get it done in two weeks because any holiday longer than that makes him feel like a lazy bum. But it all begins with Berenika texting me from Blaise's top-floor suite that she's ready for sparkling clean windows, and she hasn't done that yet.

Hang on a sec. I was just sending Justýna a 'what now' text when a message from Berenika came in. Yes! She's in there! Blaise is an utter gentleman, she says. Her multi-part reply:

We walked around for ages debating whether or not to get matching 'World's Best Mum' tattoos, then we got on to the legal system in the 14th century Caucasus, if you can fathom that

(He's been reading a Book)

Say a Georgian husband of that era found out his wife was cheating on him

He'd have 1 year from the official date of the discovery to either burn down his wife's lover's house or non-fatally injure the other guy

So many ways to take advantage of that permission; we really got into it

I asked which revenge fantasy had hit the spot.

Employing an ocarina group to follow the wife's new boy-friend around doing the 'Happy Birthday' tune all year long, she wrote, then: It's well past window cleaning time. no?

They've ordered room service, so it doesn't need to happen *now* now, but the sooner the better. Where the fuck is Vincenzo . . . OK, he's here too, grumbling about parking in this neigh-bourhood in a totally unrelatable way.

∴

Our spy-story protagonists were having a pretty lavish break-fast, all 'Try this, try this', and feeding each other as they looked out across the city's parapets and cupolas – I could see Berenika pointing out landmarks. Blaise was nodding with-out taking any of it in; Berenika was the landmark. And then there we were, the window-cleaning crew looming between them and the really rather excellent rainbow that was vault-ing across the grey-blue sky. Blaise tried to look through us: maybe that's what a gentleman does. Getting up and swishing the curtains closed would've been rude, and would probably also have given Berenika the impression that he was about to pounce on her. Blaise smiled at his breakfast companion, chewed some more *koláč* at her invitation, then glowered at his smartwatch, perhaps hoping to see an e-mail from Justýna about meeting earlier than planned. The guy basically looked anywhere and everywhere but at us two window cleaners.

Vincenzo sent a great big grin my way, and I sent one right back – *Don't worry, Blaise, you're right on time for being implicated in the dissemination of state secrets* – then I rapped on the window, pointed at Vincenzo, who was holding up his beer cooler, and beckoned Blaise. 'Welcome, Penthouse Boy!' I bawled. 'Welcome, welcome! We come to you in the spirit of European brotherhood. Did you know there's nothing better than a nice cold beer whilst admiring rainbows?'

Blaise looked at Berenika, Berenika looked back; we lipread, she was saying *Blaise, they're definitely talking to you.*

He shook his head and chuckled, amused but already en route to displeasure: *No, not me, why would you say that . . .*

'Wow,' Vincenzo said loudly. 'Wow! We're just trying to be nice, just trying to share a moment of beauty, but he doesn't want to, he thinks he's above us . . .'

We rattled our long-handled brushes against the window. 'Alright, Penthouse Boy, we see how it is! We're good enough to clean your windows, but not good enough to have a beer with!'

Blaise approached us, rotating his hands in the universal gesture for *Wait, no, let's start again, please, but from a sensible place this time.* He couldn't even hear what we were saying yet. Once he got the window open, Vincenzo stuck his head through and had a go at him: 'Are we asking you to pay for the beer, mister? Are we? *Sakra*, you penthouse people . . .'

'Acting like we asked to pick your brains about the stock market or something . . .' I added.

Blaise looked over his shoulder, but Berenika was nowhere to be seen; as expected (by us), our girl was zipping around the suite, thieving items.

'Do you – ah, do you have mineral water in that cooler?' Blaise asked.

We gave him the blankest stares we had. All I know about Vincenzo is that he has a lot of mouths to feed – seven kids, I believe – and he's an absolute pleasure to misbehave alongside.

'It's just – you know, so early,' Blaise said.

I started to reply, but Vincenzo beat me to it: 'Listen, Penthouse Boy . . . how would you like it if we came to your country and criticised you for boozing too late in the day? Try having a bit of respect for our culture . . .'

Blaise respectfully argued with us for a few more minutes. Wouldn't we run into difficulties if we were observed drinking on the job? (He indicated the other platforms juddering across the hotel's facade.) Were we sure that the beer wasn't going to harm our window-washing objectives?

'Your arm, please,' I said. He held out his arm and, quick as a flash, I tied a friendship bracelet around his wrist. 'What, what is this,' he gasped, scrabbling away at his arm as if volcanic boils were erupting all along the skin there. Heaps more neurotic than he looks, that Blaise P. He's covered the visible markers of neurosis with gym-generated muscle.

'Don't get hysterical, Penthouse Boy. We're friends now, that's all,' Vincenzo assured him, 'Good, good friends. And you ain't drinking no water with us.'

I passed Blaise a bottle of 12 per cent lager. He refused at first, but Vincenzo roared 'OH!' in a way that must have reminded him of someone terrifying. Blaise took the bottle, raised it in a toast to us, and didn't 100 per cent fail the peer-pressure test . . . his beer went unsipped. And he drifted towards the neighbouring room, saying 'Karla? Karla? You OK?'

We needed Blaise with us, not moving away, so, as previously agreed during the planning stages, I climbed up onto the platform rail and, once I'd made certain that the coast was as clear as could be, I asked Blaise why he couldn't just shut up and drink, raised my arms and, BAM, I jumped. He could see the web of wires that supported us, but probably didn't see that they were clipped to our suits, as was the harness that immediately snapped taut as I fell. From where Blaise stood, he'd seen someone launch themselves at the pavement because he'd refused alcohol before noon, and I could hear his 'WHAT THE FUCKING FUCK?' from the floor below, along with Vincenzo's admonishments: 'Look what you did! We're sensitive people! See what happens when you snub our beer?'

::

Hope you can still read this . . . I'm not in the best condition after my jump. Ribs got banged against the scaffold – it's weird, you practise so many clean swings encased in all that fall-arrest gear, but when it comes down to it, the flailing of your own arms and legs proves the biggest menace. The drop was so good this time, though, poppies . . . close to the popping of a cork. I dropped like I'd been prised loose from some too-tightness there isn't any terminology for – prised loose and tossed into a dark-red whirlpool (that could've been the wind squashing the veins in my eyeballs). There was some muscular commotion – stronger than shivering, tamer than a convulsion – I felt it five times, and, Kinga-A, you were there, and so were you, Kinga-B, and you, Kinga-D, Kinga-E and Kinga-F. All of us together in the flesh! It was like a party. Do you realise that's the only time we meet – when we think we might be done for? What if I'm trying to open this door for us, all seven at the same time; if you found out that's all I'm trying to do each week, what would you say to that? I noticed that we were only a party of six today, though. No Kinga-G. Maybe try to check on that tomorrow, Kinga-Duša.

··

Well, poppies. Blaise's flea market was quite the flop. We at Závin are having to issue the first refund in the company's history. Why this week, of all weeks?

'The first refund, but certainly not the last,' Vincenzo says. I think he thinks he's being encouraging.

We regrouped over coffee and decided that the nun's habit played no part in the fiasco – the nun's habit stays in rotation.

Blaise is observant, so he recognised me, but didn't connect me with that mortally offended window cleaner. He turned to Berenika and seemed to be about to raise the recognition issue, but then he just shrugged in an 'I'm sure it'll come back to me later' way. So that was alright.

Berenika herself is mostly in the clear; she did everything she was supposed to, leaving the crucial tote bag at reception for me to collect once I'd transformed into Sister Faustina. Berenika had bagged everything we'd asked for: the book on Blaise's bedside table, his electric toothbrush, his spare sunglasses, etc. But she'd added something we hadn't requested: a greyscale matryoshka doll. Berenika says she thought it was a cute bonus, but I didn't have a good feeling about that little knick-knack. Had I been in her place, I wouldn't have touched the thing, let alone swiped it. Its greys were deep, and the white parts even deeper . . . bottomless. An insinuating type of greyscale, this . . . after looking at it, every other pigment else seems too saturated – actually, could grey and white be the only true colours? It felt like every other colour could be some kind of sinister aberration. I didn't bring any of that up during our evaluation coffee break; it would've been the opposite of helpful.

Besides, I'm only thinking of the doll in this way after the bidding war it was at the centre of. I mean, yeah, me and that matryoshka doll did grimace at each other when I first found it in the tote bag, but I thought I was just feeling sort of woozy on account of having miscalculated my jump half an hour earlier.

The rest happened like this:

I put on my reasonably legit-looking imitations of the tunic, veil, scapular and belt of a Benedictine nun. And I loved getting ready. Before today, I think I was too embarrassed to ever mention stuff like this, but now I want to tell you . . . I'm not sure why dressing up always feels like some sort of self-coronation – it just does; the whole room sparkles with the ritual of tucking and folding heavy cloth. Must consult with Dr H about it, if I get the chance. Anyway, having completed our transformation from window cleaners into a priest and a nun, Vincenzo and I headed over to hip, hip Holešovice and got the flea market set up as quickly as we could, repelling curious students on the lookout for deals as we did so: 'Sorry, but these particular items can only be sold to virgins . . . thanks for understanding . . .' All this was standard.

Berenika led Blaise right up to the courtyard we'd commandeered, and we showed our client all the items laid out on our trestle table.

'All for a good cause,' I told him.

'Right, sister, but who's the guy watching us from behind that tree?'

(It was Vincenzo.)

'Probably a well-wisher,' I said.

Vincenzo waved. Blaise didn't wave back, and Berenika asked him if there was anything wrong. It was sort of enthralling to see all the dread and suspicion leave him when he looked at her: 'No, no . . . I just . . . for a minute I thought . . .'

He caught sight of the matryoshka doll, and it all came

rushing back; he sprang to his feet and reached for it, promising me fantastic sums for the parish fund. I should've opened that doll before setting it out . . . if I had, I'd know why he was so desperate to buy it back.

I'd just begun gussying up the asking price when a lady in a turquoise cape pranced past our PRIVATE FUNCTION sign and straight up to me. 'Hi! So it *is* you,' she said, studying my face at heinously close quarters. 'Where did you learn how to ignore people who are trying to speak to you? You're better at it than Londoners, even.' She sounded super-impressed, and she had to go. I drew myself up to my full height and stated that this was a church fundraising event. She gave me a pantomime wink.

'Say no more, my dear, say no more. Let me help out. I could buy . . . hmm, this book? No, it's in English, that's no good . . .'

She was running her hands all over Blaise's things and his agitation was palpable. Berenika couldn't do anything and Vincenzo wouldn't – I saw him shrugging and shaking his head – the lady in the cape was my problem.

'There's nothing for you here,' I told her.

She picked up the matryoshka doll and said she'd never seen such a thing done in grey and white. 'Rare and valuable,' she declared. 'This is right up my street. I'll give you 26,000 crowns for it.'

'It isn't for sale,' Blaise said, before I could.

The intruder ignored him: 'Twenty-six thou in cash for what I'm guessing is a worthy cause! Who'd refuse? Not you, surely . . .'

'It is NOT for sale,' Blaise insisted, then turned to me. 'Tell her that! Why aren't you telling her that?'

Milica shook a finger at him. 'Be quiet, young man,' she said, in English. 'Don't you know who I am? Tell him, Kinga.'

I reached up under my veil and pulled my bandeau lower down, somehow hoping to cover my whole face with it. No such luck. 'I don't know her, I swear on my life I don't know her,' I said to no one (as no one believed me).

'OK, wow. Well . . . we'll talk about this later,' the lady said to me. She told Blaise and Berenika that her name was Milica Janković. She also said she was the head of the NCA.

'What's the NCA?' I hissed.

'The Naturalised Czechs Association,' she hissed back.

'Oh yeah? And exactly how long has this Naturalised Czechs Association existed?'

'An entire morning! The paperwork was finalised today. We're having our first meeting over there' – she pointed at a building behind Vincenzo's tree – 'in half an hour. This market of yours feels pretty illegal to me, but if you can show me your permit, I'll leave you to it without reporting you. As long as I still get to buy my curiosity, that is.'

That blackmailing little hussy Milica was still holding the greyscale stacking doll as she said all this. I took it from her and told her she was the one who should show *me* a permit for her meeting. I told her that if she didn't show me a permit she was going to get kicked like a football. The others looked kind of shocked, like Ježíš Maria, *this isn't how we talk to pensioners, Kinga.* But the lady understood me at once; she's the kind of difficult person who doesn't bother trying to hide behind anything. There was no need to play the pensioner card anyway. This Milica, right . . . this Milica showed me a permit for her NCA meeting. An authentic permit, as far as I could tell – and I have seen a few.

'Are you in a mood because I didn't invite you?' Milica asked. 'I would have, but, you know, the boundaries we discussed . . .'

Poppies, I entered a state akin to buffering; I stared at Milica Janković without blinking or speaking. At first I thought I was just overwhelmed by the enmity I felt towards this woman who was fucking up my day of the week with her demands and her insinuations. My mouth, my throat – something was caving in around that area, I was aware of a cracking sensation, a split . . . either my skull or, only a smidgeon more bearable – the sky. Writing this all down now, I can barely believe how much hatred I felt. How was it that I kept still when it felt so obvious that eruption was the only way to find relief?

Someone was very firmly pinning my arms to my sides. It was one of you. That's the only explanation I can think of. If any of you want to own up to protecting this Milica person, feel free. Seriously, I won't hold a grudge against you for interfering, I'd just like to know.

Paralysed though I was, it was clear that after a few seconds Milica cottoned on to the fact that staying still increased her risk of getting a smack. She must have seen it in my eyes; her own widened as she backed away. 'Er . . . until Monday, then,' she said. And then we had to pack up our trestle table and come clean with Blaise.

Juicy J was lying on the sofa watching TV when I got home. He got all defensive when I asked what he was watching. 'I made you dinner; it's in the oven,' he said, before answering my question: 'Oh . . . it's *The Tinder Swindler*.'

I wasn't hungry. And I've watched *The Tinder Swindler* with Berenika; we'd already done all our flapping, already shaken our fists and said 'Ah, men . . . MEN . . .' whenever we felt prompted to.

Tonight, I sat down beside Juicy J and put my head on his shoulder. His arm rose and hovered. He asked, 'Is this a good idea, Kinga-Casimira?'

'Juicy J, why are you asking me? It's your hug to grant or withhold.'

He gathered me up against him. 'What's the matter? Were you thwarted today?'

'Yes!'

'Right, then,' he said into my hair. 'Who or what are we hurling abuse at tonight?'

'Milica Janković,' I said.

'Milica Janković,' he repeated. His intonation – too quick, too slow, something – made me look up at him.

'What? You know her too?'

He asked for a description of her and I gave him one.

'I'm so sorry,' he said.

'Sorry? What for, Juicy J? So you know Milica . . . that isn't anything to apologise for. After all, this city's quite the goldfish bowl.'

'Yeah, but . . . look, I'm sorry for what I'm about to say. I don't know how Milica found you, but I guess it was only a matter of time, really. Whatever it is she's done, please don't be too angry with her . . . she's honestly not that bad . . .'

Poppies: Milica is Juicy J's mother.

THURSDAY

10 a.m.:

Squad – Kinga-Duša here, reporting for Thursday duty.

First of all, Kinga-G, just in case you decide to take a look at this week's diary before you wipe us all out, I'd like to propose a deal.

Drop all the other Kingas except me.

You know it makes sense . . . I'm the only other Kinga who doesn't mind going to church. We can get along. I was about to write that I'm the only other Kinga who doesn't bite off more than she can chew, but that isn't true, is it? It's a matter of record that Ms Kinga-Alojzia Sikora's chewing abilities are on a different level. That's the very substance of my grudge against her, trivial as it sounds after I've read what was going on with the rest of you during that French holiday.

Kinga-B wanted her rights recognised, and that's fair enough. Kinga-C wanted her big sister analogue to search for her. I sympathise. I do. I wish a guardian of the days before mine would look out for me too. I've been experiencing some fairly remarkable palpitations on the left side of my head ever since I opened my eyes this morning. That's right – palpitations. It's like my ear is having a heart attack. I put a heat pad over it for fifteen minutes; hopefully that'll prevent swelling . . . or is it ice I'm meant to use . . .

Back to the topic of sacrificing Kinga-A (amongst others)

for the greater good. Squad, I've heard you out, now you hear me out. All of us are super-hush-hush about this, maybe the entire squad was in denial, but I can't be the only one who noticed how tight our clothes were after that trip we were uninvited from. I didn't entirely abandon my post, by the way. I tried to clock in every Thursday at 9 a.m., but three times somebody I assumed was Kinga-A sidled up and gave me the opposite of a pep talk, saying things like 'Oh no, give this Thursday a miss, it's *especially demanding* this week, you should let somebody else take care of it...' That sounded good to me, so I just went back to sleep. Believe me, I've learned my lesson! That woman has no concept of moderation when it comes to white bread, cheese, chocolate and whatever greasy meats caused that skin inflammation. Benek has confessed that there was an evening of ortolan consumption ... a cele- bration of recovery from Covid, he says. I say that ortolans, bread, cheese et al. are the evils that messed with the finely balanced proportions of our figure. I had to fast for months afterwards. Just black coffee and water for the months it took to get back to normal! Our leader falls over herself to label us – let's be real, this is NOT gratitude, guilt or a superiority complex, this is task delegation handled by a person with- out self-control. So I get crowned 'unbothered queen'. Yeah, well, that's probably how someone comes across when they're starved out of their mind and have to be economical with their reactions to stimuli. I'm a good Catholic who follows the teaching that though Hell exists, our Creator's mercy creates the possibility of that place being empty of human souls. So even if it isn't Hell you go to, Kinga-A, just go straight to wherever it is those who deny themselves nothing end up. Go right now.

With the exception of Kinga-G, our only innocent, I reckon the rest of you can go too.

Kinga-B is far too proud of her dubiety. And she's really fucking controlling on top of that. I don't even need to go into it – it's obvious that the conduct she admits to is just the tip of her manipulation iceberg.

Kinga-C, all you had to do was keep your hands off this guy; how could that be too much to ask? How could you make yourself the reason I wake up all intermingled with someone else's body? He was already awake, and he was ogling me in silence, with those eyes like weird citrus-coloured lamps. No inhibitions left there, what with you having fallen asleep clinging to him. It doesn't matter that no intercourse took place. You mustn't ever do anything like this again. If you do, I'll kill you myself. It's as simple as that, so don't say you weren't warned.

Kinga-E, I feel like I understand you (so you probably hate me). We're both entranced by all that's beautiful, and make no allowances whatsoever for ugliness. Or, to uncover the workings of these passions: anything we're drawn to is sublime and there's no redemption for anything we're repelled by, right? They come and go, the impressions we want and the impressions we don't want. You're prone to seizing them, Kinga-E, or pushing them away. It's as if you live for and through your yeses or your nos. Whereas I will not travel in either direction.

Not even for a thing or person I very clearly hear calling out to me. Dr Holý once asked me if this passivity could be an expression of fear. I don't think it is. I don't worry about what would happen if I enacted a yes or a no. All I know is that I'm happy where I am. Which can make a person less concerned with following impulses, I suppose.

Kinga-F, you're messier than Kinga-C. We seem to be on the same page when it comes to squad loyalty, so at least there's that. Even so . . . please leave. Every single one of you, just leave! You never stop seeking to have some sort of impact somewhere in the Badlands outside of our head . . . after all these years, none of you have learned how to lie flat and allow situations to take care of themselves.

Squad, don't you realise how thorough the Church is when it comes to cataloguing the blessed? I'm referring to the Unified Church – all branches of Orthodoxy plus the Catholics, the Anglicans, etc. Every day is a saint's day, practically every name refers to someone who's currently crowdsurfing the Heavenly Host. What I'm saying is, there's already much too much of everything, and the saint we're named after has no discernible incentive to add to the OTT actions that got her noticed in Heaven. But St Cunigunde's Day could still be an opportunity for a bit of intramural spring cleaning. We could give this squad the gift of functioning more smoothly. I've cast my votes, so now it's over to you.

∷

2 p.m.:

I ask your forgiveness for that outburst, squad. I don't think I meant most of it. I shouldn't write to you before I've taken my magnesium bath.

The truth is, Kinga-G and I could never keep this show on the road as a duo. We've never worked a day in our lives, and we're extremely unlikely to come across any sponsors more lenient than our squad members. I'll tell you what's keeping me from grovelling right now: our rock. I'm talking about our psychotherapist, Ctibor Holý. He neutralises the effects of all those muddy exchanges I sat through with other doctors. We talked at cross purposes for hours, me and those other doctors . . . I had my memories tested and tested and tested, and I happily toed those lines. You lot wanted somebody non-squad to talk to. Kinga-A wrote that it'd be like signing up for mental-health insurance, and the rest of you agreed with her. I continued the search for our non-squad collaborator, but kept being offered the learned opinion that we've got to amalgamate, that there can only be one Kinga and it's impossible for us to live happy and fulfilled lives as we are. All the doctors said so – except for Ctibor, who didn't perceive any imperative to cure us of each other, and said as much. I know he held the same information session with each of you; we told each other about it, and, until we got used to him, we were a bit incredulous, weren't we . . . ? But he's been true to his word. Unless you cherry-pick allusions to your own versions of conversations with the Doc, I'm in the dark as to what you discuss with him, and vice versa. This exceeds expectations. It's ideal.

I'm the one who brought the Doctor into our lives, so if we do have a vote, it'd be immoral to vote me out. It's also fine if you do vote me out. I'd be better off without you ungrateful bitches!

I, Kinga-Duša Sikora, have no fear of Sunday.

However this *svátek* goes, it'll be done <u>our</u> way. That's what this guy, Jarda, doesn't understand. He reminds me of this woman Kinga – I'm talking about the OG Kinga – was seeing on and off for a few months. The Parsley Pusher. On their first date, Kinga mentioned that she hates the taste of parsley, it's like eating hair. This woman was a good cook, and she became fixated on proving that she was some kind of healer of faculties, nurturing enjoyment where only disgust had existed before. Kinga would finish the main course she'd been served and then the Parsley Pusher would take her by the hand and say, *Oh, Kinga, this recipe called for bushels of the herb that you used to hate the taste of.*

Jarda has that same 'everything's different now that I'm here' smugness about him. Did you know he's convinced that she (whichever Kinga it is he thinks he's in love with) has chosen to be with him over being with us?

We had a little chat while I was running my bath – he hovered in the hallway, and I sat on the edge of the bathtub checking the water temperature with the same hand I used to stir the oils into a glossy whirlpool. I asked for a glass of wine, and he brought me one, saying 'So this is breakfast Kinga-Duša style?' as he handed it over.

'No, it's just wine, Jaroslav. How long have you been sober?'

'Three years or so.' Vague words spoken in peculiarly rigid tones. He may not have been a scrupulous timekeeper before moving to his valley of clear thinking, but this was a mark the move had made on him; he filed all his time away in detail now. I could see that the real total he was thinking of included months, days, minutes and possibly seconds too, and I watched as he bit those off and swallowed them.

'I see. What's the best thing about having made it this far?'

He took a while to decide, but settled on: 'I don't get as confused as I used to.'

'I'm glad.' I wasn't just saying that. 'And at the very beginning – how far did you think you'd make it?'

'One day. Even trying for that felt like pushing my luck. But I had lots of help.'

'From who?'

'Volunteers, professionals . . . would you like some more wine? We wouldn't want you getting thirsty, would we?'

I handed him my glass and looked over the previous pages of this notebook until he returned with my second helping. Then I said: 'So. These supportive volunteers and professionals – where exactly are they based?'

Frost and haughtiness: 'That's of no importance,' he said.

'I wish I could agree – it's so pleasant to be able to agree with people, isn't it – but I think location does matter a little bit. Especially if you met any of your guardian angels at the psychiatric facility where one of . . . where a Kinga has apparently been going for long walks.'

He shrugged. 'Kinga-Duša,' he said, 'what matters here is

this: For ages – maybe a year into this sobriety thing – getting through the day with a clear mind was almost unbearable. You know how camera phones are a bit too good now, and facial features in photos are so detailed that people's oily pores just glare out at you? It was like that, only with thinking. The clarity was too appalling to deal with, or accept, or – I don't know the word. But there was this one volunteer who made it easier not to go searching for some sort of little fuzzy jacket for my thoughts. I don't think there was any specific thing that she did, it was more . . . who she was, the way she was. Gradually it dawned on me that the days I saw her tended to be the only day of the week when I really felt like – well, me. And then she told me it was the same with her. She's like some kind of fugitive. She has to snatch days from the schedule you've so minutely divided up between you—'

I laughed. I laughed and laughed – so much I spilled wine into my bathwater. He hated that; he shouted: 'Shut up! Stop that right now! We're in love!'

Oh, my God . . . for a while it felt like I was never going to be able to catch my breath again. But I did, and as soon as I did, I tried to set him straight: 'Listen carefully, Jaroslav. Kinga Sikora isn't in love. If by some extraordinary circumstance she fell for somebody, it would never be with a person who's looking to change her.'

He went in for a bit of whataboutism: 'I'm not the one who tries to snuff Kinga out and then punishes her for fighting back,' he said, arms folded.

'Punishes her?' I asked.

'No food on Thursdays . . .'

Oh, OK. Ordinarily I'd have kept my mouth shut and simply tuned out while this knight in shining armour chided me. It's hardly a rare occurrence for us passive types. You just murmur something mollifying every and now then, and you get through it; eventually your lecturer leaves you alone. This time . . . is it possible to run out of placatory instinct? I don't know why I dug my heels in. That's not true – I do know. He sounded so sure that I'm shallow, and he's deep. As if he isn't serving the same sentence in the same cell as the rest of us. I drew my chin down so that the bathwater clasped my neck cleanly, like a collar that had had all the starch swished out of it. It was just the right outfit for delivering a sour soliloquy. I wished aloud for sight like Jaroslav's: sight that bypasses matter and surveys the true essence of a person. I'm willing to bet on the wild coincidence that every blindingly bright soul Mr Make Sure You Eat Every Day has been drawn to was housed in flesh that weighs fifty-five kilos max (if feminine). That guess about coincidental similarities between his exes is for your eyes only. I didn't actually say that to him; I praised him for seeing souls and left it there. I was more careful than I needed to be. Even if I'd said exactly what was on my mind, very little of it would have landed. But at least the challenge would have left this page, you know? He wants to ignore or forget that the interventions I make in our diet are directly linked to this body's ability to tick his tortuously simple boxes, and I want to fucking remind him.

He talked over me the entire time: '. . . And just in case she might still have the energy to take the reins back, you hit her over the head with – who's this author? Never heard of her . . .' Jaroslav gave my Mary Westmacott paperback a dirty look – 'but she sounds *dowdy*.'

Absent in the Spring is superb, but I didn't feel like summarising the story for him. No need to offer up easy ammunition by telling him I'm reading about someone who very belatedly comes to realise how heinously she's treated everyone she claims to care for.

While I was contemplating that, Jaroslav changed tack: 'What sort of person do you reckon Kinga Sikora would fall for, then?'

'Save that question for an expert or for a figure of consequence, Jaroslav . . . not for the marginal bather you see before you.'

'So I should just piss off and let you bathe in ignorance, is that what you're saying?'

'No. Telling people to go or asking them to stay . . . aside from things like that not making any difference to what you'll end up doing, I really don't care enough either way. I've let you know this isn't going to work out the way you're hoping, so the rest is up to you. Get over this delusion if you want to. Don't if you don't. Whatever works.'

Jaroslav nodded slowly. 'You don't dare kick me out,' he said. 'You know that I'm telling you the truth, and you're scared that if you try to get rid of me, Kinga – the Kinga I'm here for – will finally snap.'

This time I had to bite the inside of my cheek to keep

from bursting out into more laughter. He told me I looked as if I could do with some more wine, and I nodded. Jaroslav brought the rest of the bottle and put it on my bath tray, covering his eyes with his left hand as he did so. Then he added an empty tumbler and a carafe of water with cucumber spirals swooshing around in it like jellyfish.

'Thanks.' I would never have asked for water, but once it was in front of me, I drank it. I drank and drank and drank. 'So,' I said, once I got my mouth unstuck from the tumbler's rim, 'this Milica . . . your mother. Is she after anything in particular, or is she just extraordinarily interfering?'

'Neither. There's no way she could know about Kinga and me; she probably just likes whichever one of you she ran into. She tries to drag a soulmate my way every other month. She's . . . look, it's not fair to call my mother faddish, but she does love a clean sweep, starting all over again from the beginning, and so on. When she decided to become a citizen, she kept saying to us, do you know what humans are? Then she'd say it herself, if we wouldn't give her the answer she liked: just a bunch of smashed crockery arranged in a cabinet. And do you know what Czechness is, she'd ask? Her answer: it's blending in by standing out. She, ah, vowed to follow in the footsteps of the pair of daisies in that crazy sixties film, she was going to run wild scattering her petals . . .'

'I think I get the picture,' I said, and searched until I found his supposed girlfriend's name in my diary entry: 'So . . . you're not already seeing someone named Zdenka?'

'Zdenka? No. That'd be my brother's girlfriend. Well,

fiancée, by now, if she's accepted his proposal.'

'That doesn't sound like something Milica would sign off on . . .'

'What can I say? She's been overcompensating lately.'

'For?'

I heard Jaroslav settle onto the hallway floorboards. If he was sitting where I imagined he was sitting, we were back-to-back.

'Why are you asking about Milica? Looking to gloat over the shabby state my family's in?'

'No, Jaroslav. You might be disappointed to hear this, but you're not a threat to me. We've got too much in common. You're just like the other Kingas, you're just like everybody, walking out into a pea-soup fog every day with a plan to arrive at some dock named Tomorrow, thinking to yourself, OK, it's all pretty unlikely, but if I persevere without any detours, I just might make it in time to greet my ship as it's coming in . . .'

A look I couldn't interpret crossed that pretty face of his, then vanished double quick. Something like unease, or outright alarm? Neither reaction was one I'd set out to elicit, but that's not so puzzling. Not everyone is good at saying reassuring things. 'Our ship will come in on Sunday, Kinga-D,' he said. 'Kinga's and mine. And, sorry, I don't know how to "soften" this next part . . . you won't be here to see it.'

'Let's agree to differ, just for now. What can you tell me about Milica?' I sipped some more water; it was more refreshing than the wine. If this is indicative of brain damage, I don't mind it. 'Stop being stingy, Jaroslav. Tell all.'

Tak . . . I'm told Milica is Jaroslav's adoptive mother. She's also his biological mother, but he has trouble making room for that in his psyche due to her having discarded him when he was very young ('discarded' is his word) and only come back to claim him well into her second pregnancy. She denies that this was her way of shopping for the ultimate gift to the child she actually wanted to have – tadaaa, a big brother! – but admits that from the perspective of someone who isn't her, it really, really looks like that. Up to a certain point Jaroslav could still cut ties with his distress by way of methods that are almost academic: the factors that brought about his abandonment have been acknowledged and discussed and thought about ad nauseum. Milica's first husband was the kind of defence lawyer who was both indispensable and hated: he defended people guilty of unthinkably depraved crimes, crimes you still couldn't envisage even after hearing how they'd been committed. And the services Milica's husband provided were far from perfunctory – the man was deeply serious in his preparation of arguments that shielded monsters. She knew him well enough to understand that he didn't do this out of fascination with monstrosity, but because he had to make sure that the trials he participated in weren't show trials in any way. This first husband's trust in the law took the strange form of requiring justice to strike down any appeal for mercy or re-evaluation of evidence with no regard for the refinement of that appeal. He built baroque sandcastles for the legal process to wreck. Sometimes Milica's husband won a case, and he'd get sick when that happened. Sick to his stomach; food wouldn't stay in his system, and he'd be in a bad way until it was time to prepare for his next case. Milica was alright with living with someone like that and caring for someone like that. For the first few months of her pregnancy, she was also alright with raising a child with someone like that, but she was confronted weekly, strangers told her they hoped terrible things would happen to her and her child so she could learn not to condone evil. She came to feel she'd done evil herself, bringing Jaroslav into an environment where he didn't stand a chance. An environment that would definitely harm him in revenge for his father's sickening successes. She relinquished motherhood, she thought she was sparing the boy something, she didn't see what else to do. Her husband was relieved. She'd been the one who'd gone on about being lonely at home while he was immersed in work. It all happened the way it happened; new-born Jaroslav left in a baby box outside a gynaecology clinic. He was a summer baby – Milica's told him she watched the baby box whirring for about a minute, making sure it was working properly and keeping the child from overheating, then she got away somehow, she's not sure how she made herself leave, but she did. All of that sort of ruptures Jaroslav's ear drums, but not irreparably. The overwhelming difficulty he has in opening his heart to Milica without reservation lies in not having been told that his adoptive family was his biological family for about ten years. This is something Milica hasn't been able to explain. She located Jaroslav, turned up with her second husband in tow (a Czech guy, just as her first husband was, though J says Husband Two is much more suited to family life

– maybe even made for it) and she missed the moment when she could have begun with the truth. Maybe social services should've thought to run DNA tests . . . no, I'm not sure why I want to frame them for this madness. It's Milica's failure. I just think the misery of not telling him what she'd done must have been equal to the misery of telling him. This is about words, and choosing whether they flay you alive or turn on someone else. Telling her son the truth was a thing demanded of Milica, and after she had told it, there'd be no reviving any part of him that called her his mother, she just knew it. He found out in a worse way, via a medical emergency, but it wasn't so bad for a while, he had a drink or two to take his mind off it . . .

. . . There Jaroslav corrected himself. Making Milica the reason for his alcohol dependency is a trap he'd rather not fall into. He'd been drinking too much before he found out, and won't let himself forget that Milica orders events so that she's to blame. He told me it helps that his younger brother is such a staunch friend to him. He'll never forget his brother approaching him late one night to ask: 'What do we do? Are we abandoning her?' and gravely awaiting his command.

When he stopped talking, I was quiet for so long that he said: 'What are you doing – taking notes?'

Of course I was, squad. You've just read all my notes. That wasn't all, though. I kept tilting my wine glass and readying myself to sip from it, but at the very last moment I lowered the glass again. Not quite against my will, but . . . I wanted to drink, yet I couldn't bring myself to. Squad, someone else was with me, I was not only myself. Which one of you was behind this? Own up – unless you want me to take Jaroslav's claim that there's a different Kinga secretly working against us at face value. Hold on, hold on, it takes more than having to force myself to drink some wine to sway me. I had not closed myself off to what he was telling me, that was all. I'd identified with him, probably over-identified. It happens; semantic processing is so hasty that the finer particles (the ones that make up your 'I') are exchanged in an instant. My 'I' was on its way back, but the wine still smelled nauseatingly sweet. The slightly bitter water was better. I finished it, asked Jaroslav to bring more, and pulled the bath plug until the magnesium foam sank low enough for me to replenish the hot water without having to get out of the bath or risk overflow.

'Is it healthy to spend the entire day bathing?' he asked, slamming the refilled carafe down in front of me and stalking back out into the hallway.

'I won't be here all day; I'm meeting someone later.'

'Who?' he asked, pushing his head in through the doorway, all sharp and alert.

'No one you know.'

'An appointment, is it?'

My turn to hassle him a bit: 'Who knows you're here, Jaroslav?'

'No one,' he said, with an above-average degree of composure.

'Not even your brother?'

'Nope.'

'How are you so sure?' I asked.

'My phone's been switched off since Saturday.'

'Ah, you weren't aware that the Find My Friends and Family app still tracks the locations of devices that are switched off?'

'You're lying,' he said, with a hand to his beard.

'The set-up with the zip ties – was that tactic aimed at Kinga-Alojzia? At all of us? Or somebody else altogether? Anyhow, someone from your life outside of these walls knows you're here, yet they're leaving you to it . . .'

'You don't know what you're talking about,' he said. 'And I can give you an example.'

I took a big gulp of water. 'Go for it.'

'*Don't wake up this Thursday, it's gonna be a rough Thursday, why not let someone else deal with it* . . . remember being told that when you were in France?'

I didn't say anything, just watched him, trying to think of ways he could know about our three lost weeks without being in cahoots with the thief. Eventually it came to me: 'Oh . . . so you got cosier with Kinga-A than she let on. Well done.'

Jaroslav laughed. 'No, Kinga-A was very unhappy with me. She didn't like what I had to say about her pretending to have been in charge all that time when she has just as little idea what happened as the rest of you.'

'Alright – what really took place, then, according to you?'

'The original Kinga shook you all off and broke through. She's had enough of living like this. She wants her week back.'

'OK, listen: I don't claim to be infallible. What you're saying could be true. But even if I wanted to take this idea on board, there's just something . . . off about hearing it from – well,

128

you. If the OG Kinga wants to go back to the way things were before our deal, it'd be the simplest conversation in the world. We really are here for her, you know. All she has to say is that she wants to come back full time, we'd say OK, and that's it.'

'Oh, but she has told you, Kinga-D. She's made repeated requests. She's put up messages all over this flat, and she's sent me photos immediately afterwards. But it's starting to seem as if each of you has taken the messages down before any of the others could see . . . you all seem so clueless about each other. Kind of interesting, given that you seem so dedicated when it comes to writing to each other. More like dedicated to lying to each other, I guess.'

'Jaroslav,' I said. I was becoming unsettled on his behalf. 'If anyone's taken those messages down, it was the person who wrote them. My squad doesn't do things like that. Have you considered the possibility that your Kinga doesn't actually want you, and that this is her approach to letting you down easy? An "I'd love to, but the Executive Board says no" type thing?'

Jaroslav shook his head: 'I was warned that you're the most spiteful one . . .'

'Young man! Whoever it was you've been talking to, it can't have been any Kinga I know. I remember Kinga Sikora – the original Kinga, as you call her . . . and that isn't how she goes about her business.'

Jaroslav went all sage on me: 'People change when they're cornered for too long.'

'Did your Kinga tell you how our agreement came about?'

'Of course she did.' He didn't elaborate. A bluff . . .

I told him about the secondary-school reunion the OG Kinga attended two years after the bank transferred her to Prague. She'd just turned twenty-nine. When the invitation arrived, she saw a chance to put that lacklustre second decade of hers to bed once and for all before her third drew to an end too. She'd grown sophisticated, and could hold her head high around everybody she'd had to hide from before. It was more than the glimmering coordination of her wardrobe palette; she moved and spoke with exactitude. There were no maybes about her levels of fulfilment. Her secret sauce? *Celibacy.*

The reunion was being held at an exclusive and moss-bedecked rooftop bar in Warsaw – a setting emblematic of both her cohort's success and the brain drain their village had undergone. Kinga took the bus from Florenc, a journey that gave her over ten hours to google everybody she remembered and gloat over the turning of tables in the looks department. She boarded the bus with her hair still bundled up around giant purple rollers, did her make-up using the front camera of her phone and disembarked in top gossamer gamine form, looking like breakfast, lunch and dinner at Tiffany's. She took a cab straight to a suburban bachelor pad her brother owned and had given her the keys for – she spent half an hour there, undressing, steaming the bus-seat-generated wrinkles out of her outfit, and then pulling columns of warm fabric back onto her body. Arriving at the bar about an hour late, she had her list ready. What list? The list of people whose night would be ruined by the sight and sound of her. She'd show them just how demoralising a softly spoken 'long time no see . . .' plus a radiant smile could be. If it was at all possible, she'd go in order of the most to least convincing 'who, me?' faces that had been swivelled in her direction each time she'd caught the would-be Style Committee mocking her. It was sad that they didn't have anything else to talk about, but perhaps she just cut too much of a comical figure for a bunch of bored teenagers to move on from. It was her footwear. The flashy, jailbird's-progeny trainers that were simultaneously too expensive and too juvenile for a sixteen-year-old. The students in regular kit couldn't fathom how Kinga had obtained a dispensation to wear those trainers with LED lights in the soles. It would have been more humane not to grant the new girl such permission; bystanders were challenged to a space-laser duel with every step she took, and when she ran there was a kind of strobe-lighting effect. This was a perfect storm of unfavourable circumstances: Benek's feet being much bigger than Kinga's; Benek's immaculately maintained collection of light-up shoes bought for him by a father who picked favourites (shoes he'd already outgrown by the time he was eleven); Kinga's grandmother refusing to buy her shoes when they already had serviceable pairs worth thousands of złoty gathering dust upstairs. Could Benek's collection not be sold to buy shoes for Kinga? The answer to that was a surround-sound NO. Everybody was against it. The shoes must be kept, and what kind of big sister campaigned in favour of spoiling her brother's beautiful memories this way? Kinga Sikora was to stick her feet in those ridiculous shoes, and she was to be fastidious when cleaning them at the end of each day. She sometimes tried to take a break from being a figure of fun. If it wasn't raining or freezing, she just went barefoot instead, tiptoeing along the corridors in socks with soiled soles. But they talked about the tiptoeing too, those kids who talked about her but had some kind of horror of speaking to her. What if something they said to her was taken the wrong way, her dad heard about it and spun around in his criminal spiderweb until a strand smashed in the windows of a business establishment associated with that mouthy schoolmate's family . . . ? That's what the girl in the retro-futuristic shoes preferred to imagine her classmates thinking; she could've condoned that kind of carefulness. Really those kids were thinking of their reputations. You couldn't be seen talking to the new girl. It might look as if you were friends with her.

Time to say hello and goodbye to all those dear old nonfriends . . . Kinga strode into the bar, picked up a glass of champagne and took a look around.

She didn't see any of the people she'd shared good things with. She could never forget ballroom-dancing classes, and having to stand there wearing her third change of socks as boys sought the honour of a dance with the girls either side of her. Away they went, the giggling belles, the stoic troopers, the magnetically morose maidens, and on it went, the avoidance of the new girl, until some inexplicably gallant boy asked her to dance – asked in the right way, that was key – her two gallants asked as if they expected her to say no, I will not dance with you, but hoped to dance with her anyway. They took their own shoes off and trod all over her toes without taking any notice of their peers' coarse witticisms. Kinga liked those two, and she liked their girlfriends, who cheerfully stepped up and asked her to dance if their boyfriends were absent. It never felt like a charity effort. There were others she liked. Kids who were still writing their essays five minutes before the teacher came around for them, her spiritual twins: 'Wait, is this a complete sentence?' they'd ask her, reading back the line they'd just written. Yes, Kinga Sikora was schooled amongst a varied herd, but none of the ones she'd enjoyed being acquainted with turned up at the reunion. That type of person is never seen at that type of thing. This corresponds with the roles they played back then – only at the reunions do we understand that the presence of those who didn't adhere to popular opinion was the existential equivalent of a holograph beamed in from a dimension where school stuff is minor.

When it came to her least-favourite classmates, however, Kinga was spoiled for choice. She approached number one on her hitlist with a 'Brygida? I barely recognised you!' at the ready, but Brygida . . .

Teenaged Brygida's speciality had been making Kinga cry via methods that carried maximum deniability. Twenty-something Brygida threw her arms around Kinga and all these terms of endearment burst forth (from Brygida, of course, not from Kinga), along with many tender recollections of their friendship and all the tomfoolery they used to get up to. Kinga didn't interrupt her; her evaluation of all this cooing wavered. Brygida was on famous-sibling alert. Scratch that, Brygida was up to her old tricks, only she was trying out an even more indirect technique these days. No – this classmate of Kinga's was high on something, or delirious, or . . . Brygida actually believed what she was telling Kinga and the small crowd that was gathering around them? It was a peculiarly glutinous crowd, everyone in it was an adult rendition of a teenager she'd wished she didn't have to coexist with, and now their hands kept patting her and sticking to her, and they were saying they'd missed her and they were so glad to see her. OG Kinga's schooldays had reorganised themselves so that she'd been friends with people who would never have bothered with her. She didn't take this lying down; she protested quite strongly. But: 'She's arguing with us,' Brygida said, with an indulgent smile. 'Wow. Have you been telling people you were a pariah or something? What a brat . . .'

Kinga hurried to the bathroom and requested a group chat – you will remember the way she did it, squad, building a tower of coins, eight coins in all, and topping it off with a dog-eared Tarot card she'd pulled from her purse: the Eight of Pentacles. But I don't think you'll remember how Kinga came by that card . . . it was too far back for most of you. She was fifteen. There were only two unmarried women under the age of forty in the village where Babcia and Dziadek lived. One was Kinga's mum and the other was Gosia, who was the very picture of a nineteenth-century governess (if nineteenth-century governesses had discovered miniskirts and bared their shapely thighs with gravitas). The village lotharios catcalled Kinga's mum, but didn't bother Gosia at all. She looked good enough to eat, kept to herself and lived with an orange cockatoo named Fanfarone

– there were definitely invisible strings attached there, and some debate as to whether there was also a Rottweiler on Gosia's premises. It seemed likely that the cockatoo barked like a Rottweiler at night, but you can never be too sure. Anyway . . . from the moment Kinga's mother and Gosia ran into each other at the greengrocer's, they only had eyes for each other. Kinga's mum got stuck in without preamble: 'What on earth is a city girl like you doing here, miles from anywhere?' Gosia said she needed to be in a place where a certain man would never think to look for her, and the friends exchanged glances that struck Kinga as analogous to crossing themselves. For a few months, Kinga saw a lot of Gosia. Gosia lent the girl clothes and books, and would have solved the shoe problem if not for the differing shoe-size issue. She offered her face as a canvas for Kinga's efforts as a make-up artist. Gosia also asked Kinga to engage her cockatoo in conversation. 'Fanfarone was SO uncouth before he had you to speak with,' she'd say, shaking her head. Kinga didn't feel like she was doing much to improve Fanfarone's communication skills; their exchanges were based on word association, and the cockatoo kept surprising her. When Gosia eventually deemed it safe to go job-hunting in the city, Kinga helped her pack, holding up items and discussing them with Fanfarone and trying to keep the mood buoyant even though she knew she'd miss Gosia and her cockatoo. If Gosia's offer to tell her fortune was intended as a diversion from gloomy thoughts, it worked.

'Oh no,' Kinga said. 'Don't tell me. I'd rather just get through it when it comes.'

Gosia laughed at her. 'Do you really think it's going to be that bad? No, shush, I'm going to tell you, just quickly, wham, we'll put it all on one card.'

She unbundled a deck of cards from some purple gauze they'd been wrapped in, had Kinga hold them for a moment, then plucked one card from the centre and said, 'Ah . . . OK.'

It was the Eight of Pentacles. She handed it to Kinga and said, 'Well, there you go.'

Kinga looked at the image. An apprentice hammering away at a set of discs – shields – coins? She shrugged. 'See? Nothing special,' she said. 'I told you.'

Gosia gave no immediate reply; her packing strategy involved running around the room sweeping things off shelves and straight into boxes she'd already padded out with textiles. So Kinga had to check that she was right, waving the card like a sports referee: 'Gosia. Hello? This card means something bad, doesn't it?'

Gosia told her it was fifty-fifty. 'It might – but only might – mean that you're fated to work really hard your whole life, with your only reward being the work itself. But that's good, I think. That the reward actually exists, you know? And that it's possible for you to receive it. Even better – you won't be alone.'

'I . . . won't?'

Gosia tutted. 'Come on, Kinga. Nobody is. Far too many have this terrible feeling of being cut off from the rest of humanity. But what it really is, girl, is that our lives wobble around so much we don't really stand a chance of conducting a proper head count in between ups and downs.'

At the time Kinga's reaction was *Ugh, alright, Gosia's cheesy farewell includes a message about how we're all connected*, but I think Gosia was referring to the fact that there are at least eight of everybody. Eight is the minimum. She just didn't want to come out and say it because she could see that Kinga was already troubled by the prediction of never-ending toil. Gosia was wise to the seven of us, I'm sure of it. That's part of what makes it so apt that we were all able to gather around when Kinga stacked the coins and the card.

And there, in that onyx-tiled seventeenth-floor bathroom where the muzak was so loud it drowned out the sounds of the toilets flushing, the seven of us took over. We'd been with Kinga for ages, taking charge when she floundered, and she'd resume operations when she was ready. This time she just told us: *Guys, would you mind just being me? I mean, what have I even been doing it for? I thought I got to make my own revisions, but this . . .*

She placed her days into our hands and went away without a backward glance. We thought it was temporary, but we haven't heard from her since.

'And that was, what, a decade ago?' Jaroslav asked.

'Just over a decade. You seem to think we love being in command, and it is nice a lot of the time . . . I'm not going to say I hate getting facials, I love that stuff . . . but our priority is not letting this individual go to waste, for want of a better way to put it.'

Our Romeo hadn't been privy to any of that, and hasn't been offered alternative background; it was visible in his face.

He made an abrupt retreat, mumbling that he had no further questions. Amen . . .

I stayed in the bathtub to write this – the paper's damp, so my lettering's puffing out and blurring as I spin ink along the page. Kinga-A may be happy to assume leadership status (and the hassles that go with it) but I'm the oldest of us. I carry the memory of learning to walk . . . you know me, I wanted to stick with crawling. Standing upright felt like overdoing things. The view before us wobbled out of balance and wobbled again and again . . . but there were even greater excesses to come: the slap slap slap of our feet rushing forward – there was no brake, we just zoomed until we dropped.

I don't mean to taunt you with firsts you weren't there for. These things are coming up as I try to think about Kinga and Jaroslav, what there is between them. Aside from first steps, I've only been this wired once before. It was dinnertime at the flat in Poznań; Kinga was twelve, and her dad still lived with us, but it was almost time for him to go to prison. The air was fuzzy with panic – something very dark afoot, and not just the smoke from burned potatoes. Six-year-old Benek was candid with him: 'Why did you cook? You don't know how to do it.' Kinga's dad answered that he wanted dinner to be extraordinary today; it might be our last meal together for a long, long time, but of course that wasn't up to him, it was up to our mother. He looked at Kinga's mother, who'd set the dinner table, taken her seat and was watching her children with a vacant smile, as if she wasn't seeing or hearing any of them. For about a month – or two months – before this, there had been rows between the parentals. Their rows were usually frightening ones that often involving the smashing of crockery, etc, but these latest rows were conducted in whispers; there was no possibility of listening in with any accuracy. It was something to do with Kinga's mother refusing to declare that Kinga's father had been with her at such-and-such a time on such-and-such a date. Kinga kept hearing her mother saying *I can't. I'm really sorry, I can't. Because if you did this, if you really did this . . .*

Then her father cooked that dinner and brought the plates out and set them down in front of everybody, and he poured out Sprite for everybody too – Benek was so overjoyed by this he punched the air and shouted YESSS – Sprite was his favourite but he was hardly ever allowed it because of boring stuff like dental health. He grabbed his glass, but their mother emerged from her trance – in what felt like the blink of an eye she was leaning over her son, her hands wrapped around his, saying 'No!'

We observed without touching our own glasses, or the blackened mound of food on our plate. Kinga's dad observed too, and he sat equally still. He began talking about the importance of staying together as a family. He was out of his mind, really – the more he talked, the less he was able to hide it. The thought of being behind bars while this snake in the grass could see his children every day, go anywhere with them, probably find them an upstanding father figure . . . all that was a torment to him, and he couldn't hold it in. It'd be much better for them all to go away together, wouldn't it? He wanted them to agree. They didn't agree. Benek didn't want his Sprite any more. And that same night they left for Babcia and Dziadek's house – Kinga, Benek, their mother and a friend of their mother's whose name I'm sorry to have forgotten, since she bundled those three into her car and drove all night without stopping. I'd know her face if I saw her again, and that will have to do.

The platform we're on is revolving, squad, just like it did back then.

∴∴

I'm at U Malého Glena getting my basement-blues fix. All listeners are shadows in this cave, merging with the riffs; the music accumulates in the pitted walls like moss. This is where I ended up after going to Dr Holý's office. He wasn't there. You don't even have to knock; all you have to do is look at his door. It holds a diamond-shaped hollow of glass that's lit up when he's in. If he's out, bleak diamond, grim diamond, dreary diamond. Once I got outside the building I called him, he answered the phone, and it's starting to look as if he's not going to change his mind about making me look for a new doctor. He reminded me that he'd agreed to maintain phone contact until I find someone else, and he won't see me until then either. I have the list of colleagues he's recommended. I suppose I'll start the search again next week.

Jaroslav asked me who I think Kinga would be in love with if not him. A rhetorical question, probably, but I can answer him from here: she'd fall for someone who won't cross any lines. Staying away from someone you care about is an alien notion to the likes of Jaroslav.

Jaroslav: I'd better avoid that one. Otherwise I may say or do something that isn't fair. Almost a year ago, I asked one of you for help with my painful confusion over Ctibor Holý. In the message, which I asked her to delete, I said that I thought I might be getting attached to someone. What if this is a good thing, I asked. It didn't feel bad – certain glances, certain silences sent me off on sweet, strange flicker-spin, like some mad little bat flapping around a stained-glass chapel at dawn. I didn't say all that, I just said I thought I might be getting attached and it didn't feel bad. The Kinga I confided in deleted my message, as I'd asked. And I deleted her message, as she'd asked. I won't name her; I'm not saying this to cast her in an ugly light. Without proof either way, I'll repeat the reply I received.

So what? So what if you think something is happening? It isn't. There's no getting attached for you, even if you want that. You'd never be the one who lets us all down.

I'm not saying I disagree, or that I would have preferred a message about following my heart. All of this has something to do with that pesky declaration I've heard Snoop Dogg make so many times. Fun fact: whenever I'm especially pissed off with our leader, I listen to those affirmations she's so fond of starting her day with, and I rank them from most to least ludicrous until there's a change in mood that reminds me of making up with Benek after a fight, the way he and Kinga would hand each other letters of apology along with red pens so that they could amend and discuss each point of the apologies until they either reached a settlement or burst out laughing, or both. As I listen to the Monday-morning affirmations, groaning from the base of my diaphragm all the way through, the affirmation that stands out as daftest switches places from week to week. But I've noticed that every time I listen, *My feelings matter* always emerges as the most tolerable notion. It isn't Jarda's fault if the line between *My feelings matter* and *My feelings are the priority* makes no sense to him, and it isn't my fault if holding that line is all that makes sense to me. Let Kinga's Romeo be happy if he can.

I'll close this notebook in a moment; I'm staying here until closing time. Hopefully he'll be asleep by the time I get home.

FRIDAY

I'm dictating this as I walk around, a bit out of breath due to rage and other physiological factors, so the microphone or listening-and-transcription program or programs or whatever might mishear . . . I'm dictating punctuation marks, too, and if the settings work properly, when I'm either screaming or howling the words should appear in capital letters, so here we go—

Kinga-Duša, I've got to start with you.

If, after propositioning our therapist (or whatever it was you did to make him run for his life) you feel like you have anything remotely resembling a right to open your mouth and speak about how disposable the rest of us are . . . if that's really how you feel, Kinga-D, all I can really say is LOL.

That was going to be my entire entry for today, just completely washing my hands of you, this, and us. Apparently, I'm too stupidly soppy to just leave the rest of you to your fate. This morning I did Kinga-D's favourite thing, to see if it helped me get into her mindset. Bathing gets on my nerves – it takes ages and there's all this selective soaking of different body parts. Afterwards you're not really sure if everything went the way it should have, liquid creeps out of your ear as if it's a slug that's appalled, simply appalled, by what it's discovered, and you can't make up your mind whether you want to cry into your towel or have a gigantic sneeze. It's basically baptism all over again. Showering is so much less regressive, but the before-and-during-and-after-ness of a bath acted as a sort of Rosetta Stone for me . . . Kinga-D, I took another look at your diary entry, and the words swept me aside one more time, tidying me away so that I didn't face it directly. I'm turning towards it anyway: that lightless diamond in the doorway. The one you don't want us smudging. Well, alright, we won't! Or, speaking for myself: *I* won't. Now you give me something, Kinga-D . . . something more than this clinical witness to your passion. How about half a hint as to the where and when of all this? I'm halfway to making up my mind that this is your prideful way of letting us know that all this steam you're blowing around is one-sided and the doctor has never looked at you the way you'd like him to. But I don't know. I just don't know. I feel like I should know what your silences mean, and yet how can I? You aren't me. None of you are. You're rolling your eyes like, did the dimwit only just catch up? The thing is, 'knowing' the extent to which I'm not any of you is quite distinct from <u>knowing</u>. The former is a chalk line and the latter is an electric fence.

But Kinga-D, my dear sister in Cunigundacity . . . this erotic/romantic transference story with the doctor . . . surely you see how basic it is. Unless you've let Hitchcock's visuals persuade you that there's some kind of glamour to latching on to someone who takes a vocational and/or generously remunerated interest in what goes on in your head. If that's not what this is about, I'm at a total loss. How can someone like you have feelings for a guy like that? A guy who's always fumbling around for something – with his hands, with his mind. Speaking of online meetings, the ones I've had with your doctor (OK, our doctor) couldn't be more different from the ones with my perfumer. Once, I silently watched as, apparently unaware that he'd accepted my video call, Dr H spent eight and a half minutes shifting a stethoscope around his ribcage, listening for, and apparently failing to detect, the workings of the pump in his chest. It's like that when you listen too hard. Kinga-D, I don't mind telling you what most astonished me here: I got the distinct impression that your boyfriend seemed relieved he couldn't find any evidence of his pulse. The vibe was <u>very</u> prison guard dutifully putting on a show of inspecting the grounds for a prisoner he'd helped to escape, you know? Like . . . *I'm searching, that's my job, but I'd better not find him, he'd better be gone, if he isn't gone, I'm fucked beyond belief.* Eventually I cleared my throat and told him his camera was on. He looked up – he didn't jump, or exhibit even a hint of nervousness – he thanked me for joining him and the session began. And just as usual, he did all those little things that make it difficult for me to derive benefit from speaking with him. Fake drinking, for example. During pauses in our conversations, he lifts his cup, sort of massages the area just above it with his lips, sets the cup down with a satisfied look, lifts it again . . . maybe this gives him a feeling of actually having imbibed some flavourless, odourless fuel. But I can't look at that without getting so aggravated that I lose the thread of whatever we were talking about. Ctibor Holý is not a person who exults in the sight, sound, touch, taste or feel of anything. I hope you at least have

145

some inkling of that, my dear sister. Your doctor isn't a person who is willing or able to take what his senses have to offer, full stop. But maybe you see gentleness where I see joylessness. Huh, is this . . . have his feelings for Kinga-D worn him down? I'm trying to remember how he was when we first met him. Could it be that he's dejected not only because he's involved in a serious moral infringement, but because his partner in crime can only share the burden on Thursdays?

Shit. Now I feel bad for diminishing what may be happening between the two of you.

But that doesn't mean I'm letting you off. Any of you. I'm going to shrink all your feelings like you've shrunk mine. You think I don't know that you disregard my diary entries? I've tested this in various ways: I wrote so many questionable things that none of you questioned. Probably the biggest whopper was the entry where I claimed to have tried to make a donation at the Motol blood bank, only to be turned away when a doctor found that our blood type has inexplicably changed from O to B negative. Not even nuclear radiation does that to people. But does that announcement of mine ring a bell? Of course it doesn't. Nobody asked 'Hey, what's going on, are we OK, how could our blood type have changed?' Nobody offered to check again, because none of you had even so much as skimmed the entry in the first place. I'm one of the jobless ones; a person who isn't contributing to the rent can't possibly account for her day in a worthwhile manner. But I'm not the only one who spices up the actual course of events with things that didn't happen. Kinga-B and the candle wax in her hair . . .

I don't think we got the full story. Aside from Kingas C and D being too lazy/busy to change our linens, how else would it be possible for me to observe that the top right corner of our fitted sheet is singed this week? I'm guessing one of us did some firefighting in the early morning, but either couldn't remember, or wasn't able to tell the rest of us. We don't like that, do we, we don't like the intermediary period between Kingas . . . we'd rather tell some story that constructs accountability for every last unit of our time. One good thing about our current crisis is that anyone who makes it to Monday will finally pay equal attention (or equal inattention) to every single one of our entries.

So, with my spotlight guaranteed, what I want to tell you is this: I was never under the impression that our life was perfect. Still, it was good. We were doing alright – we were freer and more fortunate than we had any reason to expect. We were finding our way, realising what can and can't be done with a day. Each one of us working that out for herself. And increasingly, our happiness was less and less reliant on what other people think, say, or try to do about our arrangement . . .

For some reason – ARGH, quickly blowing my nose, I'm not fucking crying, not that I ever cry, and not that you care, it's the cold activating my mucus, I'm so fucking angry with you and with this weather – for some reason you weren't content with what we have. Turns out Benek isn't the only gifted actor in the family after all! And apparently you think some sort of shabby tragedy would suit us better. One of you is secretly shimmying amongst us, trying to get us to turn against each other so comprehensively that we end up exchanging everything we are for that <u>beast</u> who's taken over our sitting-room sofa. Maybe there's more than one bad apple. It could be three or four of you, carrying some bizarre type of shame about not being the overtly sustained focus of somebody else's desire. Honestly, I could shake you.

But I've never liked sore losers. I don't want to start being one – not so close to the end, anyway. If this is the end. So . . . whichever of you is behind this, congrats. I choose to shake your hand. Continuing to plead the case for the seven of us is beneath me. Beneath <u>us</u>, really. You've won! Please enjoy abject domesticity with HIM. (You won't find that creature's name staining any part of my diary entry.) If I have to choose between repeating this morning and disappearing from the face of this earth, I'll take the latter.

I know how to spend a Friday. You're meant to wake up at around 11 a.m., get some coffee going, sign for all our packages and open them with a mellow piano rendition of the *Nutcracker Suite* playing so that Christmas morning lasts until 2 p.m. (because you're taking breaks to run your nose along a piece of perfumed card, or along your own arm, slowly and surely tracing all the different facets blended together in one fragrance and taking notes). Then you have a late lunch, write and post a review to your perfume club's blog. After that, you see who's around to go and see something at the cinema, or you go for a drink with a few of your darlings. You dote and are doted on, you analyse enigmatic epiphanies and petty disputes with the same focus normally applied to international incidents, someone walks you home because the two of you still have some laughter left to discharge, you're home just before midnight and more often than not you go to bed happy. That's a normal Friday if I'm not on Muse Duty. I am on Muse Duty today, so I had to skip everything after signing for packages, anyway . . . but still.

The morning began with the bedroom curtains ripped open and HIM standing between the sunlight and our bed. His voice was curtness itself: 'Get up – you've got errands to run.'

I asked what time it was, and then I asked who he was and what he was doing here. Everything was a different hue of mauve – it was really strange – I knew this could not be the case (why would it, it's never been the case before) but it was like swimming around at the bottom of a glass of wine. I felt like this had to be a problem with my eyes, so I screwed them shut and opened them again, did some eyeball gymnastics until all the other colours re-entered the room and HE was the only thing that remained mauve. Which was fitting, as he was the only feature of our bedroom that shouldn't have been there at all. But even he stopped being mauve and went back to his usual colouring when he spoke again, in answer to my questions: 'It's seven thirty, I'm—' he said his loathsome name, and I asked for his surname.

'Why – do you want to google me or something?'

'No, I thought – I just thought that if your full name rang a bell, it'd help resolve this issue.'

'What I'm doing here, Kinga-Eliška—' (He paused because

149

I'd sort of yelped; the world had been mauve and then it wasn't, plus I couldn't comprehend how someone I'd only just met not only knew me as Kinga, but as Kinga-E) – 'You alright there? Finished screaming, or is there any more to come?'

'No, that was it.'

'Good. What I'm doing here is teetering on the brink of being betrayed, I fear.'

I asked him to give me five minutes, got up, took our diary into the bathroom and locked the door. I read everything, Kingas A to D. Certain pages had their corners folded. Unless any of you have suddenly got into the habit of doing that, I regret to inform you that HE's read our diary entries, all of ours, going months back – probably looking for some mention of him, which of course he won't have been able to find before this week. There can't be any other reason for the darkness of his mood, his deeds and words.

I got dressed and made my way to the sitting room, which had become a kind of smog chamber; HE was sitting on the sofa beside an incense burner that was pushing out spirals of smoke. It wasn't the kind of incense burned in churches or temples; this odour was stupefyingly fresh. Some variant of mint that clustered like algae, forming tingly membranes over the links between what I could see, what I could smell, what I could taste and what I could hear – the divisions were nowhere to be found. The air was giving my teeth a good brushing, except that my teeth were my ears. You get the idea.

I sat down in the armchair across from the sofa. He came over – at least I think he did – it was very difficult to see him.

Throughout our conversation, such as it was, I found him very difficult to see – he was a murky mist that handed me a cup of tea and warned me that it was hot.

'You've read that Kinga-C left some negatives with her friend Tonda, right?' he said. (He was back on the sofa again. If he'd ever left the sofa, even.)

'Yeah,' I said, blowing on the tea.

'Drink,' he said.

'Give me a minute.'

'Oh, right – just like the five minutes you asked me to give you hours ago? I think not. Have some now.'

'OK . . .' I sip-slurped some tea, and heard him take a sip from his own cup too.

'See, isn't this nice?' he said. 'A quiet and civilised morning. After tea you'll go and get those photos, and you'll post them to the address I've put in the pocket of your coat. The coat nearest the door; you can't miss it. There's a note to send with the photos, and someone will pick it up from Tonda's place at 4 p.m. I've made it really simple for you to stick to our plan.'

'Our plan?'

'Not mine and yours – mine and Kinga's.'

'Right. It's horrible, isn't it,' I said. 'Having doubts about whether things are going to work out as agreed. Looking for a way to stay calm.'

I'd intended to expand on that, but couldn't. This was not because of the tea – a mint tea so metallic that it glinted as it struck my tongue – and it wasn't because of the incense. I was overwhelmed by the two together.

'Thank – fuck for . . . that,' he said. 'The – herbs-are-kicking-in.'

Not being able to say 'Herbs?' any more, I tried to think 'Herbs?' but didn't even manage that; all I could do was hold onto my teacup as HE told me we wouldn't be talking as much today. 'Less talking . . . means less – lying. S'beller . . . for boffffffffus . . .' I couldn't see a clock, but it felt as if it took him at least an hour to enunciate all those words.

Then, get this: just as soon as we'd both been stripped of the ability to vocalise anything at all, the doorbell rang. The first delivery of the day. My perfumer times the sending of this 3ml of fragrance so that when I meet him later, I will already have been wearing it for four and a half hours. He's never late to a meeting, and I'm never late with my fragrance spritzing. I get the package, I rip open the package, the rest of the day races towards his reaction.

The woman at the door was not the usual courier. She was dark-haired, and looked to be one of the haughtier components of the retiree demographic – actually, maybe she wasn't haughty. She was smiling amicably, but she had aristocratic bone structure, so she couldn't help looking sort of above it all. Perhaps she could've helped the way she was holding my perfumer's envelope, though. It was dangling from her gloved fingertips as if she couldn't wait to be rid of it.

'Good morning,' she said. 'Can you sign for this?'

Wordlessly, I signed our name, took the envelope, waved at her and began closing the door. She hindered that process with her foot and, smiling ever more sweetly, said something about it being funny how much trust people have in spray bottles being labelled correctly and without deceit. 'I never wear perfume myself,' she said. 'Just imagine – buying something in a shop or in the post and then just spraying it all over yourself without a second thought. People are so trusting. What if it was a nerve agent? Did you read about what happened in Salisbury, that little English town? Honestly, no one's safe . . . oooh, are you starting the weekend early, dear? A little dry ice or some such thing, to get the party going?'

She peered into the billowing mist behind me.

I was silent, HE was silent (what else could we be, what with the tea and the incense?) and, suddenly severe, she told me, 'Now listen, dear, I'm going to have to come in for a moment.'

I shook my head and kicked at her foot, which only budged a very little. She was flexible, too, keeping one foot in place while the rest of her wriggled in through the gap in the door. She explained herself as she did so: she was looking for somebody, an unforgivably insolent young man who'd shoulder-checked her on Národní třída a few days ago while she was struggling along with her groceries. She'd almost dropped the bags, she told me. There'd been a dozen eggs in there, almost a raw omelette served up on the pavement . . . not to mention the scrambling of her nerves and her blood pressure and her human dignity. But the young man hadn't apologised, or even looked back, he'd just sauntered onwards like the star of some music video. Unluckily for him he'd enraged a lady who was well-connected. She'd been asking around about him, and he'd been traced back to this very building . . . If I'd been able to speak, I would naturally have been asking a lot of questions very loudly – scratch that, if I'd been able to speak, Siri would've already dialled 112 for me. Siblings . . . how to convey the distress of words being locked away when I most needed them? I was very, very close to flinging my head straight at the nearest wall, but I knew it'd only hurt without helping.

The courier charged past me and into the living room, where HE sat stock still as she looked him over. And when I tell you he looked <u>apoplectic</u> . . .

He must've been shouting inside his head, and striving to shout aloud. A vein stood out on his neck, and another between his eyebrows; the courier stared at him, nose to nose – she pulled a measuring tape out of her pocket and measured the breadth of his jaw. She made the most of his reluctance to exert physical force against her by pulling up his top lip and ogling his teeth, muttering to herself, 'Is this him?' She took out her phone, tapped the screen until she found the photo she wanted, held it up to his face and looked at it, then looked at him. He went from looking angry to looking . . . worried, alarmed? The photo was indisputably in his likeness; it was either a photo of him or of his doppelganger. I gasped, coughed out about one tenth of a syllable, but the courier peered at him one more time, took an equally pensive look at the photo, said: 'Well . . . the search continues. Thanks anyway . . .'

She left very quietly, closing the front door behind her.

HE found a pen, took the envelope in which today's 3ml of perfume had arrived and scrawled *run* on the back of it. When it was my turn with the pen, considering time to be of the essence, I chose to write *where* rather than something like *why*.

Tonda, he wrote, then let the pen drop and stumbled around the flat, opening windows and waving the incense away, trying to get his voice back before I left. He didn't manage that – I threw my coat on, grabbed our diary and ran.

Of course, I took a look at the note in my coat pocket as soon as I was safely seated on the tram. Very old-fashioned . . . each letter cut from a different magazine: YOU KNOW WHAT TO DO, along with an astronomical cash figure, the date of our saint's day this year, a time (15:00) and map coordinates that corresponded with a clearing in a Prague 6 nature park.

I took this note over to Tonda's. There are cleverer things I could have done, cleverer things I could be doing instead – you don't need to tell me that. But I'm not interested in being cleverer than the Kinga who got us into all this, whichever one she is. I'm seventy to seventy-five per cent sure that we don't want the same things, but I mean to help her anyway. I believe she'll tell us all about it later, maybe a long, long time from now. *Tak*: I got on a bus headed for Smíchov, and by the time I got there, my voice was back. It was very interesting to see the kind of person you consider a friend, Kinga-C. Out he stepped, and . . . what's going on with Tonda? I couldn't work out what season he thinks we're in. He was wearing socks, sandals, a pair of a bike shorts and a shearling jacket draped over his bare chest and the brash thrust of his pot belly. He didn't smell too good, either. Better than I expected, but still not . . .

good. He smelled of ever-so-slightly acidic leather. The type of cologne worn by bar-hoppers who say they hate materialistic people yet seem to spend a lot of time seeking them out; it's a scent that replicates the interior of a brand-new and very expensive car. I'm less exasperated by those who try to stimulate attraction with the scent of chocolate. If we must set traps, let's do it with bait we can actually afford.

Your chum was blasting a track by Vladimir 518 at full volume, and he had company – about ten people sitting on his sitting-room floor in a circle, all clad only in their underwear, all holding hands and chanting in unsmiling unison with V518: *Nemám pro tebe lék, nemám, nemám pro tebe lék.*

'We're holding a séance,' Tonda told me.

'Right. Well, I'll be out of your way just as soon as I get those photos, then, Tonda.'

He narrowed his eyes. 'I'd hoped you'd lend a hand.'

'Well – who are you summoning?'

'The guy we're listening to right now,' he said, then turned away from me for a moment to bounce around with his hands up, repeating the warning that was rumbling the room: *I've got no medicine for you, I've got no medicine for you.*

I'm not going to lie . . . I do have a soft spot for Vladimir 518. For a minute or so, we both listened to the realest of our city's real ones pour vitriol on aspiration scams that pathologise inequality on the level of the individual. Vote for X, book motivational sessions with Y, <u>or</u> emulate the lifestyle of Z and you'll be cured of your disadvantage! V518 and his crew have only ever seen schemes like that make people sick in ways they weren't before, and sorry, *jako*, if that isn't what you want to hear.

But . . . I hated to ask, and almost preferred to hover on the threshold of mourning: 'Is . . . has Vladimir 518 passed away?'

Tonda placed a finger over my lips: 'Of course he fucking hasn't. Why jinx him like that? No, he doesn't check his Instagram DMs, and we're just looking to ask his advice on a few things . . .'

I checked Tondy-boy's pupils for any sign that he was high. They were normal, and the whites of his eyes were creamy-clean. He appeared to be superlatively well rested. I wished him the best of luck with summoning the spirit of someone who was still alive, and almost went away without saying anything else. But your friend is unexpectedly reliable, Kinga-C. He went into his study and came out with an envelope stuffed with the photos of That Man looking pretty convincingly kidnapped. He didn't make any comment on the pictures, just kissed me on both cheeks and said he'd text me later to share wisdom from 518. Then he tiptoed back into his sitting room and shut the door and went on with the invocations: *I've got no medicine for you, I've got no . . .*

The rest was easy: I took the ransom note from my pocket and sealed it into the same envelope as the photos, and—

I just looked out of the window. A man on a motorbike has pulled up across the street. More in a bit: I'm going to ask if he's here for this envelope.

∶∶

He was.

::

Now I'm at Petřín, walking around and between the bare rose bushes. Off-season this garden really scares me – the gnarled shrubs stoop over the soil with their branches clenched, defending vacant hollows. You can feel that this wasn't a fair fight. Autumn and winter are deranged predators that rip softness away from every skinny little twig that ever reached out for something to hold. And we look the other way because we're charmed by the multicoloured leaves followed by the ice skating and whatnot. Really I think my fear for this garden must be recreational or something. There's no need to worry. The rose gardeners stand guard; I've glimpsed them checking and testing and treating their charges really early in the morning, before the funicular even begins running. Then there's this garden's position at the very top of the hill. It gets all the sky a garden can get – all of the wind, sleet and hail, but rain and sun are gathered in too, so that the roses resurrect like rocket blasts. This is where the one last man I have in mind asked me to meet him for the first time. And this is where we're supposed to be meeting two hours from now. I might still meet him . . . I just sat down on a bench and I'm watching a wiry jogger pumping his arms to no avail as he loses a race with a dog that looks like an oversized cocktail sausage on legs and gallops like Red Rum. They're crackling along the Observatory's outer walls like a fresco uncovered by history and then submerged again. The man I'm supposed to meet soon just messaged me. Again. He's already sent six messages today. I haven't read any of them. I'm probably going to ghost him, aren't I? That's just the way things are going. Not my preference, but oh well . . .

Hold on. Let me try and talk myself out of it. Failing that, it'd be nice to make myself see why I will not be here waiting for him by the time he arrives.

Right, then. A reason not to ghost him:

I've already invested whole slabs of my Fridays into this thing with him. If he and I don't meet today, and I don't get any more Fridays after this, thirteen and a half months of e-mails and voice notes will have led nowhere. And what about the bathroom mirror photos? No, not nudes. Nothing so candid. The misted-over mirrors in those photos carry messages daubed with wet digits moments after showering. He started it: the first four photos arrived without excuse or explanation. As I looked at them in turn, something oscillated in me. Something greedy . . . but not an emptiness, an engorgement. Like having a second tongue with a thicker, rougher root, and much more horned hungers. To tell you the truth, it was hard to understand what that tongue wished to speak of. Is D.C. really all that sexy? Is anybody? If it turned out that receiving those photos from D.C. triggered some sort of brain seizure that I sexed up so as not to panic about dying, that version would make more sense to me.

This world of dew, he'd written. Each word of that sentence on a different hotel bathroom mirror. He hadn't bothered to tidy away all the little clues one agonises over: yes, it's not ideal to be trying to work out whether or not someone is married based on the items that haven't been removed from the bathroom sink area before a photo was taken, but until the day every married person is so honest that you can just ask about it and get a straight and truthful answer, anyone with a crush is also a visual-media detective. A couple of Fridays later, having decided that he seemed single enough, I responded with a slapdash mirror shot: *Isaworldofdew*. I had a hunch that sending pictures of a mirror in the same austere bathroom over the course of five weeks would do the opposite of entice, so I preferred to do it all in one go. I didn't hear from him for a month: I zoomed in on every aspect of all five photos in the series, trying to work out what I had missed and what he might have discovered. Then he sent another photo. In a bathroom that was somehow both pastel and baroque, he'd exploded the letters of the word *and* so that it splintered the mist from corner to corner. The word *yet* had been left to me, and I took three weeks this time, one giant letter composed of slippery slashes per week. If you came across these photos, you'd probably feel very little, but to me that mirror-writing is us severing droplet from droplet to whisper to each other through water. The mirror photos are what Kinga-F's album of dick pics would be if she'd collected them for actual stimulation value.

We're even more restrained in person. Even when it's just the two of us he's as courteous as if a chaperone is present, perfectly deferential towards my personal space until it's time to briefly enter it. He produces a vial, holds it aloft with an unspoken 'abracadabra', and operates its atomiser. Scent settles on my skin. D.C. waits without making any small talk at all. He just exhales and exhales. So do I. Then I crane my neck in the direction he so very softly requests, I close my eyes and he breathes me in. It's for work, it's for a fragrance he's creating. I'm just a cloud of scent molecules to him. Whenever I steal a glance at him, he's looking somewhere else, founding extrapolations on the data he's gathering. In short, it probably isn't possible to ghost someone I've already been enghosted by, so I might as well . . . actively haunt him?

Reasons to ghost him:

I don't think I like him. By this I suppose I mean that if I liked him, I would know about it, the way my liking for Jas rippled in all those winters ago, as soon as she lied about what perfume she was wearing. She was standing behind me in a Christmas market queue for *trdelník*, so I smelled her before I saw her. It was a fragrance I'd know anywhere . . . sort of eau de haute couture: if it were clothing, you'd have to wear it with your chin tilted all the way up, owning your singularity before the question of whether the outfit is wearing you even enters anybody's thoughts. As for the aroma itself – for me, it's like a white and yellow garland, a slightly disturbing one, as some of the flowers are freshness incarnate and others are dead and dried, crumbling away with a sweet heaviness, not so much dust as powdered honey. In perfume terms it's possible to say you've pulled off wearing something like this if you don't hear any complaints about your scent being 'too strong' or giving people headaches. On her it smelled so much better than the pastry we were queuing for. I leaped on the impulse to tell her – tell her what? How rare she was? How do conversations like that even go? I turned around to find out. The woman behind me was brown – South Asian brown – and seemed both short and tall. One of those compact types whose brow, neck and limbs are nonetheless composed of long, sweeping lines. She shot me this sepia-ink stare that said *Don't you start, OK?* I lost about a quarter of my nerve. I knew the name of the fragrance she was wearing, and I knew which fragrance house it was from (Songes, the house of Annick Goutal), but as we eyed each other, I could feel that it would be a mistake to let on that I knew those things. Now that I'd turned around and the fragrant stranger was so clearly prepared to fend off unsolicited commentary on her existence from a random white lady, I made sure I did my bit. In English, as there could be no doubt that we were both imports. It wasn't just about looks. Czechs never allow themselves to be spotted stuffing their faces with *trdelník*. I'll try to remember that now that we're citizens . . .

Anyway, I gave this woman a tiny wave orchestrated entirely by anxiety and told her, in tones as snide as snide could be, that her perfume was really nice. I'd despaired of this exchange before it had even begun, so her reaction was . . . unexpected. Out came a genial smile, and an 'Oh! Thank you so much!'

I nodded, turned away, then, curious about the sudden graciousness, I turned back to her. 'So what perfume is that?' I asked. 'Can I buy it here, or can you only get it abroad?'

'Don't worry, I'll tell you everything,' she said. 'Don't you want to make a note? So you don't forget.'

'Right, right . . .' I got out my phone and opened the necessary app, ready to type out *Songes, Annick Goutal.*

She looked skyward for a moment, then: 'It's called Bic Nuit,' she drawled.

Song, I typed, changed that to *Bic,* then ground to a halt. 'Sorry . . . did you say . . . *Bic Nuit?*'

We made eye contact – completely carefree on her side. 'That's right,' the liar lied. 'Do you want me to spell it for you?'

'No, I can spell "Bic Nuit", thanks. I just think it would be more helpful if you told me the truth.'

Her smile didn't change. 'Look, I realise that probably wasn't what you were expecting to hear. A lot of people think Bic only ever made pens. But they released a few fragrances in the late eighties. This one's hard to find, but I bet if you looked on Aukro—'

'Ylang-ylang, tangerine, cloves and aniseed. Velvety, with a metallic edge to it. A bowl of custard topped with flakes of gold.'

I'd never seen someone scowl and smile at the same time before; it was Jas who showed me that this can be done. 'I'm afraid I don't—'

'That's what Bic Nuit smells like. No giddy indoles from jasmine and gardenia in the foreground, no frangipani giggling at the back like in the perfume you're actually wearing. So! You're taunting me. Wearing one ylang-ylang masterpiece and claiming to be wearing another that's even less accessible . . . what's going on here – multi-level gatekeeping? Does this make you feel like the queen of fibbers or something? What's wrong with you?'

The *Songes* wearer took a deep breath and then expelled the air she'd just taken in with a decisive, birthday-candle-extinguishing-style puff. After that, with a look of great seriousness, she pulled off one of her mittens. I immediately pulled off one of mine, too. Because if she dared hit me . . .

That wasn't it. She held out her hand, and warmed mine by shaking it a few times as we told each other our names and the start dates of our infatuation with ylang-ylang. Fragrance was a furtive joy until Jas, and then, in swift succession, my introductions to Cornelia, Nad'a, HaYoon and Matej. Maybe that's how it was for all of us Ylang-Gangsters. A night-blooming flower has climbed vines ranging across incalculable distances, and it's drawn us all into the very thing we have the most fear of and distaste for: a group hug. Groan all you like ('Whyyyy does she have to mention people we'll never meet and wouldn't get on with even if we did?') but this is my diary entry. You've got to let me mention my friends by name. The compound effect of that tea and incense slammed me so hard my thoughts crumpled, but they're smoothening out now, and it seems to me that it's not my siblings – or not only my siblings – I'm talking to right now. I suspect I'm saying all this by way of leaving a trace, however faint, for descendants of ours. Descendants isn't quite the right word. I don't mean people whose existence has been brought about by us in any way, I'm talking about . . . somebody, or several someones in a body, who needs to hear from an antecedent of theirs.

164

Hear ye, hear ye: there's no disgrace in reiteration. Let it be known that in the Year of Our Lord 2024, seven variants of a single Kinga were out and about, tasting such life as was available to them, and sharing the feast with friends. (In my mind I'm stating this in bardlike tenor, from the midst of a cloak that touches the ground.)

My first Zoom meeting with Mr Mirror-Writer was almost a fiasco. He showed up for it wearing a medical mask, which he refused to remove. *You're not in my bubble, I'm not in yours, and this can't work if we begin with the illusion that we wouldn't need these masks if we were in the same room,* that's what I thought I sort of half heard him say. His voice was muffled by his mask, and then muffled again by the microphone of a phone he'd positioned so far away that I kept defaulting to my automatic reaction to any unclear image that appears on a screen – the 'zoom in' finger flick. I couldn't see him properly, and I couldn't hear him properly, except for the bit where he shouted that he was going to end the call unless I put a mask on too, so we spent most of that meeting alternating between short written messages and long silent periods of glaring into the camera. *Think about the intentions you're signalling when you approach a stranger with your face uncovered at a time like this,* he wrote.

'OK, I'm sorry,' I said, and put a mask on. 'Listen . . . I don't want to fabricate an image of trust either. I think we're working towards the same thing from separate angles.'

'What? Could you speak up, please?' he said.

I repeated myself, D.C. said 'What?' again, so I typed what I'd said and sent it.

A common goal, eh? he wrote back. *That being?*

An antidote to falsehood.

He shook his head, but gave the camera a thumbs-up. I didn't know how to interpret that, and I must not have needed to know, since the conversation continued. That was the main thing, even though we clash almost all the time. For instance, I don't blog about perfumes that I haven't paid money for, and he keeps trying to get me to break that rule: 'Assessing pleasures according to a rubric of whether or not you got your money's worth doesn't confer as much integrity as you think it does,' he tells me. Have I ever seen my perfumer smile, even once? When I picture his face, he's sneering.

None of this is what I signed up for. It was pocket money I was after . . . I'd spent every last koruna of the not-so-generous books and perfume allowance you working Kingas throw my way, Matiere Premiere had just released a new iris fragrance, every other fraghead I knew was awaiting free decants from their less-broke associates, and I was desperate to circum-navigate the planet of blue-violet gauze I just knew Aurélien Guichard had bottled especially for us.

So I had a little look on Jobs.cz.

Czech-language jobs, yes, Polish-language jobs, yes. English-language jobs – now, that's where the crazy Matiere Premiere money would really be. After that I selected 'Work from Home'. And, of course, the listing that drew my first and hastiest click was the one that offered payment in perfume and self-esteem alone.

He took the ad down once he had what he wanted, but at

the time I copy-pasted it into a message to Jas. (I'm sending this entry to Jas as a bunch of voice messages, so in honour of the sacred odours that bind me and her, she'll have done another copy-paste job in turn before she prints it all out):

- I am a relatively experienced perfumer at the age of thirty-four. One day I will be a master perfumer. If I continue to work hard and avoid holidays, I think this will take around thirty years. Which is good, because I hate rushing. Mastery of my craft is all I'm really interested in.

- This position is open to all, with one restriction concerning age and one concerning diet. The first is very simple and will keep us out of various forms of legal and ethical danger: I think it would be best for those under eighteen to wait until their skin's pH is more stable.

- Next: no vegetarians, no keto dieters. I don't compose in the abstract. Each fragrance I've signed as a solo perfumer has been made for a person who yawns, sleeps, sweats, etc. Someone who's alive in the same delicate, coarse and all-too-perishable way as the fruit, flowers, herbs or synthetic accord I want to concentrate on. I want a liquid likeness that includes a deliberate and accurate count of eyelashes, blades of grass, and I'm not happy with the scent until the notes are so well blended that it is not possible to distinguish which parts of nature they're singing about. I trust my subconscious implicitly, though it frustrates me with its shyness. When it does have something to say to me, it goes all out. I know that I've found the right person for my new perfume when, having first encountered that person in a mundane setting, they begin to visit me in my sleep, and befriend me in dreams.

- My selection process begins with a line or two from you. I'm thinking of naming this fragrance 'Sacrifice'. Tell me: does any such concept exist for you? If so, in what way/s? Within seven business days of receiving your message, I will contact you to let you know if you've progressed to the next stage.

- I don't think it would be right to place an economic value on inspiration (plain Czech: you won't be paid for your time). I own many very good fragrances, quite a few from yesteryear that can only otherwise be smelled at conservatoires like the Osmothèque in Versailles. For as long as we are working on this new fragrance together, everything I have is yours. I'll show you what I have, and you can try anything you like. I will also give you a lot of newly released perfume. This could be a nice opportunity to further train your nose.

- Your tasks will be limited to wearing drafts of the fragrance at certain times and making your own notes when I can't be present. Otherwise, we'll go for

walks, we'll discuss impersonal topics, we'll forage
for mushrooms and pick cherries together. I'll cross
the seasons at your side. I'll make my own tests of the
fragrance drafts too. None of these will be laboratory-
based. In total all of this will take a maximum of seven
hours per week, scheduled to your convenience.

• You have my word that nothing inappropriate will
occur. All ten of my previous muses have given
permission for me to pass on their contact information
to my chosen candidate. You, Muse 11 of (possibly)
1011, can video-call your predecessors or meet them
in person at your leisure before advising me of your
decision. And I'll be grateful for your reference once
our project is complete.

    D.C.N.

D.C.N. stands for Dinh Châu Ngô. Pages on various niche-
brand websites came up when I googled him. All his profile
photos are sleek and greyscale – not dissimilar to charcoal
rubbings, or . . . portraits on tombstones. I might not have
lingered on his face otherwise. The brands he's worked with
have taken turns at styling him and describing him in a manner that suggests he exists only to have created that particular
company's juice, so D.C.'s online image is that of a face half
memorised and half forgotten. But when you break free from
the concept that he's infused a few millilitres of alcohol with
the power to turn our cells back into stardust, translate our

souls into sonnets or transform our flesh into sinful salad (no, really – that's from the copy for the third fragrance he got to put his name to, a composition with a hemlock note at its heart), even a peacock-feather hat sported at a raffish angle can't distract you from the fundamentals: D.C.'s features are very, very ordinary, and his eyes are alight with a cheerful 'let's fix it' rationality.

I'd sent Jas the text of D.C.'s ad so that we could enjoy his obnoxiousness in tandem. She went further than that: she submitted her own application.

D.C. approved of Jas's concept of sacrifice. I don't know what she told him it is; if she'd ever told me, I'd tell you, since I'm blabbing today. I can tell you that he didn't approve of my concept of sacrifice – it was essentially a rant. I sent him a photograph of a panel of pacifists at the 1981 International Women's Peace Conference. Everyone in the photo looks fed up and uncomfortable; one panellist has been crowded into a seat behind the other participants at the table (despite it being a long table, with more than enough room further along it). Each panellist is sitting behind a plaque with a name on it, but it looks as if there are two tiers of participant, and the members of the sacrificial tier have to sit further away from their name-plaques even though it wasn't necessary and it's hard to imagine anyone asking them to do that. You see the name-plaque and then, not seeing the person it refers to, you have to examine the image until, there she is, at the back. That's sacrifice, a calculated abdication of self as a substitute for being or doing. In this case, inaccurately calculated, but still. I told D.C. I don't want to smell like sacrifice. I stressed (probably not convincingly) that I'm not against international gatherings for peace and I don't condemn anybody who wouldn't baulk at putting the good of the world before the good of their country, etc. But you can never convince me to trail the scent of that wherever I go. The world has an insatiable need to be saved, we refuse to accept that there's some point at which it'll be time for all the matter that this world is made of to be redistributed, and so for the maddeningly temporary good of this world, its smaller components are demolished, leaving everyone morose (at best) like the panellists in the photo. That's sacrifice, and it isn't a virtue I aspire to; it's something I'll only go along with if there really isn't any other way. I think those were all my main points concerning sacrifice.

D.C. wrote back: *Oh dear . . . thank you for this answer.* He was not at all pleased with what I'd sent him, but he wanted to talk about it later, and I was choosing to see that as a promising sign. Being willing to return to the topic after he'd cooled down meant that our opposition wasn't an unbearable one, and might not even be inherent. Jas was surprised to hear that discord had already arisen over the name of D.C.'s new fragrance. She kept saying things like: 'Really? Huh, I haven't had any disagreements with him yet. Wonder what it means . . .'

And then I'd retort with things like, 'Why be coy, Jas? Just say you're soulmates and go.'

This contest for influence didn't put as much of a strain on our relationship as I'd feared it might. Moths en route to getting fried by the same flame don't really see each other as competition. We moved up through D.C.'s rankings together; we did so well that he said he couldn't decide which one of us his fragrance needed. He put both of us in touch with his former muses, and expressed the expectation that after talking to our predecessors, one of us would decide this muse thing wasn't for her. He was right. After we interviewed the muses, Jas panicked and packed it in.

I was there when it happened. I report this at the risk of Jas revising my memories to bring them more in line with her own: that's life. We'd picked five names from the list of ten, and we made our video calls together, chatting across criss-crossed time zones for most of that Friday. All five enthusiastically recommended the muse experience. Only Alma, D.C.'s ninth muse, had a caveat. She was the only one who'd become a perfumer herself: 'An unwelcome development that I resisted for quite some time,' she told us. 'But never mind; here we are.'

Alma's on the other side of the counter now. Molecules are her muses. She blends them in her lab, and she's more interested in their totalities than D.C. ever was in hers. All the way from her sun-drenched balcony in Rio de Janeiro she reminded us of what we'd already observed about D.C.'s compositions: he doesn't layer intricately, he takes one top note, one heart note, one base note and that's that. Out of all the hours D.C. spends with someone, out of all those arguments and agreements and mingling of moods, he selects a single moment, splices that moment and makes his perfume out of that speck. 'I guess what I mean to say is, don't expect to recognise the result . . .'

That was it for Jas. She broke it to me as soon as Alma had gone: 'Kinga, this muse thing is all yours, if you still want it. The give–take ratio really isn't to my liking here.'

'Huh, can you say more? Is this about control?'

'Actually, no. Out of all this intense bonding he produces something so . . . anonymous that even the person it came from doesn't recognise it?'

I shrugged.

'How are you OK with this?' she asked. 'Are you thinking that you're not like all the other muses?'

'Ha,' I said. 'Is that what *you'd* been thinking until now?'

Her reply – no, her frankness about what it was she wanted to do to and with D.C. – touched an uncanny chord. I understood why he couldn't (or didn't) differentiate between me and her.

Over the course of a month, video calls had been replaced by long in-transit conversations as we rode to the end of randomly selected tramlines together. D.C. took a seat next to a stranger and I took a seat directly behind D.C., also with a stranger next to me. He turned to face me, and we debated the most heart-melting instance of Shahrukh Khan and Kajol falling in love on-screen. This shouldn't really have been possible, since I'd never seen a film that featured either actor, but we streamed clips on his phone. I had time to form opinions, too; once we reached the end of the tramline, we boarded another tram and went all the way back to the beginning again, shivering with the thrill of vicarious romance and quarrelling with each other's rankings, I mean quarrelling with real 'how can you really think that, are you INSANE' animosity. Soon enough our seatmates discovered they preferred to go and stand in an area where there was slightly less risk of getting caught up in a shouting match.

The day after taking the tram with me, D.C. rode to the end of another line and back with Jas, only the agenda was an amiable ranking of Astaire and Rogers films. Those voyages across the city were followed by joint participation in an outdoor yoga class for me and flower shopping for Jas: she helped him assemble a bouquet for a person whose sensitivity he both respected and greatly disliked: 'But she can't know I don't like her. I can't afford to let her know . . .'

Our perfumer had observed both of us situationally, and his instincts were probably telling him that there was something if not exactly predatory, then definitely <u>aggressive</u> in our approach to musehood. We were on a mission to impregnate. 'I want that man to have my baby,' Jas said. 'My fragrance baby, you know? I want it to be my idea as much as it is his, I want the result to be the way it is not because he made some super-critical extract out of some image of me, but because I planted something of my own in him. And I want it to be dangerous for him, I want the perfume he makes to be so singular that there's no way to bring it into the world without pain. He has to feel this perfume is putting him at risk of fucking fatality; if the perfume he makes "for me" doesn't feel like that, then as far as I'm concerned, he has no muse.' With some effort, I kept myself from nodding. I felt that procreative push as an outsized tongue lolling out of my loins, but Jas didn't need any such lurid sensations. I suppose academics are tidier that way.

Is there anything else D.C. and I have in common, aside from Jas and a susceptibility to scent? Yes! The loves of our lives favoured lavender. D.C.'s grandma worked in the accounts department of a grand millinery for sixty-five years before dying her hair pale purple, having her prescription lenses tinted to match and then swanning off into regal retirement on a Moravian lavender farm, where she gained a significant social-media following for her lavender-focused beauty tips. She left the farm to D.C. in her will, and she's the reason he's going to name his perfume 'Sacrifice'. He'd asked her what a fragrance made with lavender from her farm should be called, and 'Sacrifice' had been her instant reply. 'She was kind of a married nun,' D.C. said.

We were walking around in the lavender as he spoke about the lady who'd dedicated herself to its care. She'd married a man who doted on her, and had been fond of him too, especially since this husband understood that the lavender came first. Something about D.C.'s tone of voice and the way he was choosing his words suggested that he felt we were being overheard by her.

The lavender hedges at D.C.'s farm grow to about hip height, and whorls of silver-tinged indigo throng so thickly within each hedge that they form avenues that stand like sculptures. D.C. reached out over his side of a hedge – I reached out too, we estimated that we'd need two more arms each for our index fingers to even touch, so we made do with sweeping our hands along the tops of the flowers, sweeping stems together so that the scent of all the bluish balm between us surged his way and then mine. It was more or less an exchange of kisses. Better than that, maybe. Even more of an inundation.

I told him that I, too, had known and loved a kind of married nun. I wouldn't say that Dziadek was all that understanding of Babcia's detachment, but he did accept that it was futile to demand any more than he got from her. Maybe they're all married to spiritual bigamists, all those neighbourhood uncle types who get back from the pub on a Saturday evening to find dinner waiting and their Sunday best washed and ironed. I don't believe the rest of you can miss Babcia the way I miss her; she didn't hug you as much. I'd made a resigned hugger of her by ignoring the *Get off me*s, as well as her attempts to wriggle out of my embrace or chill me by standing immobile. Our grandmother smelled divine, and I can only link that with the lavender medicinally, for what she called her 'condition'. I don't know what that tincture of hers was supposed to improve, correct or manifest – she wouldn't say, she only made sure to take her tablespoonful of superdiluted lavender extract before bed. That's a lot of lavender over the years. I used to picture its properties fanning out all along her veins, spreading into every single strand of her hair. She never bought perfume – she'd never waste money on such things: *How much?! You could buy a pair of pigs with that. Not even dead ones, a young and frisky couple, ready for breeding* . . . that was our Babcia. The one who never bought perfume, and immediately sold any that had been purchased just for her. If she knew what I spend on my smelly waters, I think she'd question our biological relationship. D.C. asked me to say more about her – in what way was she a married nun, he wanted to know. I told him she was the only person I've ever met who doesn't do anything else when the radio is on. She'd put the radio on, sit down and listen intently, refusing to let a single word get by her, and, wanting to be like that, I sat at her feet and heard nothing of what was said on the radio because being close to that woman was like being enfolded in an aurora borealis – waves and clouds of sleepy brightness. It took me years to realise that this was the closest I was going to get to understanding the way our Babcia thought and felt. All we knew of her past was that until she married the hand-some, placid builder who would become our Dziadek, she was a notable member of Lublin's affluent set, a descendant of banking heirs and salt-mine owners, the sort of person whose name on a guest list guaranteed the significance of an event. After the choice of husband that broke her father's heart and got her disowned and all the rest of it, she was a dinner lady at our village school until it was time to collect her pension. What did we want her to say about any of that?

Dziadek was just a little bit more forthcoming with us. Not much more, but from him Benek and I learned that he and Babcia had met at her family home. Dziadek been part of the team that was renovating the house's South Wing (it still blows my mind to think that our Babcia grew up in a winged house . . .) and the first daughter of the house kept showing up at break time with snacks and tea. She told them these were tokens of appreciation from her father, but one day her mother caught her and asked if this could be 'discussed' in private, and after that this break-time angel was much more surreptitious with the tea and the snacks. The men Dziadek worked with were very excited by these developments; if a woman like Babcia wanted to have fun with men like them, well, they wanted to have fun too. Dziadek only thought: *Heads will roll over these smiles and snacks and little compliments. Heads will roll, but not mine. Not over some woman who's trying to make honest men lose their jobs because she's bored.* He didn't touch a single snack she brought. He worked straight through break time, without even looking over at the rest of his crew. He slept better than he ever had in his life because he didn't have energy left at the end of the day. But there were a number of days – nine, he counted – that the bold beauty didn't appear with her basket full of treats he'd never tasted. He found that he hated this absence of hers more than he'd ever hated anything or anyone in his life. The day that she reappeared, he instructed himself not to react, and he almost kept his promise to himself until she came up to him with the last piece of *szarlotka* and said she'd kept it for him. She also asked if he was mentally OK: 'I mean, I hope so. Not wishing hard times on you or anything. It just looks like you might have a screw loose there, working this hard on somebody else's house.' And he grabbed her hand and told her his name and said he didn't like *szarlotka*, what he really liked was *napoleonka*, he was just like John Paul II in that he could eat eighteen pieces of napoleon cake at one sitting.

'Is that right?' said younger Babcia, with her hands on her hips.

'Yes, it is,' said younger Dziadek. 'You should make a whole *napoleonka*, just for me, to make up for missing nine break times.'

Babcia kept saying 'Is that right?' and Dziadek kept blurting out stuff that wouldn't have gone down at all well if he hadn't been Babcia's chief reason for wanting to treat the builders, and thus were their fates sealed. Aside from that one-time and one-time-only retelling from Dziadek, our grandparents never seemed to think about those days much, if at all. Each year, Babcia and Dziadek marked their wedding anniversary with mostly unsentimental updates to a summary she'd suggested they begin after the first twelve months: the pros and cons of getting divorced. The cons list was often one and a half times as long as the pros, but I remember there being a couple of years when my stomach dropped until the final count; I was hearing more pros than usual, and it would turn out that the cons list only outnumbered the pros by one or two points. Reading between the lines of their suspense-generating anniversary dinner chat, I reckon that Babcia and Dziadek didn't mind the trouble they'd brought each other. They were madly in love. Which isn't to say that being madly in love wasn't hard on them – every now and again there was a bit more madness than there was love.

It seemed certain that the undiscussed events before and after leaving home had hardened Babcia in many ways, but in other ways she was girlish; she socialised with her environment.

I mean . . . Babcia prayed a lot, she prayed almost all the time unless she was listening to the radio, she prayed the rosary out loud and she prayed silently while doing the laundry and so on. I asked her what she was praying for, and she'd come back at me with 'Nothing,' or 'I'm praying for my real granddaughter, who would never think it's OK to ask someone what they pray for.' But once, just to shut me up, she told me how lovely everything was for her while she was praying. *Everything finds me. The story of everything around me just comes through, loud and clear. That's the most I can say about this; now leave it, alright?* To call her prayerful state recreational is to belittle it. But I can't think of anything else that made her as happy as tuning in to the world the way she was able to, following the chronicles of all that exists and has existed and will exist with the lavender light of her attention. Sometimes I wonder if I'm like that too, except that my channel is perfume. And then I fucking snap out of it.

Dinh Châu just messaged me, and I read the message this time. He's letting me know that he's in the funicular cabin that's gliding up the hill right now. Very soon he'll be standing beside this very bench with his hands in his pockets. We'll watch the sun douse the city in the luminous yolk of a firebird as it drops into darkness, we'll get into his car and drive East along dimmed roads, surrounded by maximalist walls of 1980s sound, courtesy of D.C.'s CD player. This is what I want, anyway. I'm going to ask Dinh Châu to take me to his lavender farm. I'm going to say it's urgent. If he doesn't want to, or if he says he can't, then I'm off to Jas's place.

It's like I was standing behind a cordon, spectating. Some-one (Babcia? Someone from the day that follows Sunday?) has lifted the rope and let me pass into a decision. Most likely I was the one who authorised passage. Isn't this the crux of what we're having to deal with here? Not just that there are at least seven Kingas, but that within those seven there are another seven 'more wicked than herself', and very few amongst the seven times seven times seven agree on what to do, and how. Well, I'm the only one here right now, and I'm not going home tonight. Let HIM fend for himself.

Dinh Châu's here—

SATURDAY

Alright, Special Ks – there are only about three hours left until our Saturday is over. I'm too wired to even think about sleeping, and I know you'll be wanting to hear what went on today.

Excuse the sloppy handwriting . . . I don't want to do any dictation, as our dear Jari Bear would definitely hear it all, so I'm writing as fast as I can. Our saint's day might arrive mid-sentence, so if the meaning of anything I'm saying is suddenly amended, you'll know the reason why.

Now then . . . this morning. I joggled into wakefulness like I always do. Not sure what that's about: I must not exist in any steady state on my days off. It's like I'm some kind of flare, racing around and getting faster and faster until this brain decides to either slam the brakes or become crazed, and then – I'm here, sane as can be (lol).

I was very slow to open my eyes today. It was the first time in years and years that I haven't woken up at our place. I could feel the difference – the bed was lower than ours and positioned at an unfamiliar angle, the linens were heavier, the pillows thinner – and I was thinking about it, like, *What have you done now, Kinga-E? Where has that nose of yours led you, and how come you didn't have the civility to get yourself home before the weekend came?* I might've had things to do and people to see today. It's true that I didn't, but it's wrong to assume.

I could hear a recorded violin concerto: the volume was low, but the fidelity of the recording was so high that it put me on edge. It messes with whatever sense of spatial awareness I have when I hear the violinist emptying their lungs – or is that the breathing of the bow? Hearing that when there aren't any visuals that match up with the sound is difficult to endure without entering some kind of illusory state. Case in point: the violin music this morning had me convinced that somebody else was in the room, very softly taking air in and letting it out, and looking at me. Not intrusive looking, not even particularly curious, no eagerness to see what I was about to do or say: simply looking. The breathing was so even.

I cracked the old eyelids open by degrees – and found I was alone in a room with a closed door. There was a speaker placed on top of the shelf beside the wardrobe; that was what had created the sensation of a violin or violinist practically exhaling into my ear. It was quite a papal room, in some ways: all the textiles and furniture neat and plain at the same time as being a kind of delirium of luxury, every item silently shaped by the master of some craft. But here's the main papal feature: everything in the room was a different shade of jewel-like purple, except our diary, which was sitting on the bedside table with the printout of yesterday's entry tucked in between the right pages. I ask forgiveness from the Special Ks who put their backs into getting us through Tuesday to Thursday – I really had to throw together a cheat-sheet for immediate priorities, so I read two entries: Monday's and yesterday's. Once I'd read those, I punched the air.

Kinga-E . . . well done you. Your crush brought us back to his farm! You asked him for something and he didn't say no. That's the good news.

The bad news? Call me naive, but I don't think there is any. I got up and put on some amethyst-coloured pyjamas and slippers. Mindful of being a good guest, I knocked on my side of the door before opening it. I heard someone call out, but not from the adjoining room – they were further away. So out I went. It wasn't a big house, but somehow there was a lot of it. The rooms and corridors were lined with shelves – not encased ledges, but irregularly spaced strokes of wood that dashed across the brick walls like lines drawn freestyle on blank paper. The items on each shelf stood to attention in single file: books, rocks dutifully serving as bookends, bottles and bottles and bottles of perfume, all of those bottles small and square-shaped with handwritten labels, and more speakers – never fewer than two on each shelf. A row of skylights ran above, each one covered with a parchment-coloured blind drawn over it so that the sunlight cast these soft rays of antiquity over everything it touched . . . hang on. I'm a bit uneasy here. Is this really how I think about the things I see? It feels borrowed. But I can't think who would've lent it to me.

Because of the trail of speakers, noise condensed and coursed along ahead of me; the soundscape changed from violin music to a kind of mottled dialogue. Someone was watching a film and sharing its voices with the rest of the house. Everyone in this film was male, and everyone was as strange as war can make those who have to obey its commandments. For quite a few minutes I wandered around this ageless museum of a house listening to men talking, making jokes, voicing apathy, bellowing coercive prompts, speaking without hope – I heard one voice crackle with fear and fascination as it asked: *Are you an evil spirit?* After a while, I heard a voice that was not an actor's – it was Kinga-E's crush, calling out 'Are you OK? Let me know if I should come to you.'

I replied that it was alright, that we had all day (that's what I thought at the time, wasn't it) and that he should just enjoy the film he was watching.

'Oh, this?' he shouted. 'I must've seen it a hundred times by now.'

'Still – there were probably parts of it you missed before, so don't miss those parts again on my account. I'll catch up with you soon, D.C.'

'Mr Ngô,' I heard him say.

'What?'

'I'm Mr Ngô to you. And no informal speech with me, either.'

I found breakfast in a kitchen that looked out onto serene thickets of lavender (Kinga-A, it was a smooth, smooth coffee from a cafe-standard machine and some buttered noodles with poppyseed sprinkled on top) before I found Mr Ngô. I don't care how much and how far the rest of you are going to drag me for saying this: I think it was only possible for him to be found once his absorption in the film he was watching had slipped. He was screening it in a multifunction room of sorts – there was a fridge and a massage table in one corner, another corner was crammed with beanbags, and Mr Ngô was seated behind a desk in what looked like the office corner. By the time we were both in the same room, he wasn't watching the moving images projected onto the wall in front of him any more; he was testing perfume from two tiny spray bottles by way of balancing a tester strip across the bridge of his nose and turning his head from side to side. He picked up his fountain pen, wrote down a word or two in a notebook, then went back to the tester strips. And he looked – well, Special Ks, it was a first impression that had a few stages to it. I had been expecting someone ordinary-looking. That's what Kinga-E told us, after all. Was she bragging? *Oh, I come across faces like this all the time.* Really? Where?

Seriously, let me know. I want dates, exact locations and names, if you know them. Because I've never seen anyone who looks or moves like him anywhere.

For the other Special Ks: our fragrant friend is a few centimetres shorter than us, bulkier of frame than we are. The flare of his nostrils is too fiery to be truly modern; he's got this face full of restless crests and curlicues; for all I know, he could quite easily have been summoned out of a shower of sparks in order to contradict all orthodoxies. I said hello, and he didn't say anything, just delivered a walloper of a stare. I can't remember the last time I was looked at with such unequivocal animosity.

We were both wearing pairs of his pyjamas – mine were the spares. He'd just washed his hair and hadn't given it a thorough towelling; shimmering orbs of water kept rolling along the sleek black strands, breaking when he shook them away. You'd think someone who makes a living the way he does would worry more about catching colds and not being able to smell anything for weeks. Well, he wasn't at all. He was a full-body snarl. This almost distracted me from the detail that he wanted to protect: he was sad. And there was some connection between his sadness and his laying eyes on yours truly.

Perhaps I should get over myself. Perhaps it was just a coincidence. As far as I could tell, he'd been happy only a moment before, though, evaluating the contents of his vials and making his notes. Standing outside the door, with those olfactory activities of his audible yet invisible to me, I heard him murmuring, summarising the report his nose had delivered. He'd thought the scent was close to completion, but now he could smell that he was 'miles off . . . hundreds and hundreds of miles'. And he honestly sounded kind of overjoyed about it.

I could relate. This is the high more addictive than success (whatever success is): an objective so impossibly far off that growing old is growing towards a distance that revises the passage, measurement and even the very meaning of time with its beckoning.

Then I'd put my head around the door and his spirits had lowered. His stare was perfect, but his hands gave him away. Any student of unhappiness recognises that tightening of fingers around any comfort that pre-dates and promises to outlast the trouble you're in, whether the comforter is somebody else's hand or a liquid quatrain of an ode to lavender. And that was what he did, he locked his fingers around his tiny glass bottle. This perfumer is beautiful and he is sad, and even after seeing all the sights assigned to the itinerary of life as our father's daughter and our brother's sister, I'm still clearly very, very slow to learn that some results really do not vary (the hair-raising nothingness that comes of offering yourself up to the sad and the beautiful, for instance) because, exactly like an imbecile, your Ms. Saturday forthwith began to wonder how to get the perfumer to feel better.

I asked him about the film that I'd heard him watching. He told me it was called *Merry Christmas, Mr Lawrence*, and that all the characters were either prisoners of war from the Allied Forces or officers of the Japanese military. Their masculinity stands aghast, all its codes of conduct are scrambled – the existence of any camaraderie with their jailers cannot be considered sane and must not be demonstrated, yet hatred cannot be decisively expressed either. The terrors of this limbo howl through every hollow of their bodies; it's plain to see on their faces. Having trained themselves to exist through action, feeling has become a condition you do something about. In the camp, though, stripped of their power to protect and their power to destroy, they can do nothing but feel. Watching people go through something like that, retaining their bravery as they lose their minds (or parts of them, anyway) – it's not something you can really call sad, beautiful, dark or whatever. It just sort of burns your eyes . . . ? *Merry Christmas, Mr Lawrence* wouldn't be my top choice for a date-night film, but I suppose Mr Ngô isn't trying to date you. Kinga-E's perfumer had a plan to watch this film with her, but there hadn't been time last night.

'Why wasn't there time? What were you two up to, eh?'

Another glare from Mr Ngô. He insists that he and Kinga-E were talking, only talking.

'Oh yeah? What about?'

'Tuberose,' he said.

'Anything else?'

He was silent. After some wheedling, he grudgingly disclosed that a friend of Kinga-E's had sent him a file in the very early hours of this morning. And he'd printed it out for me. Because his muse had asked him to.

'So did you have feelings for her, or what?'

He threw his miniature spray bottles from hand to hand, clink clink, as he decided whether or not that was something I deserved to know. Six clinks later, he nodded, yes.

'What kind of feelings?'

'Hard to say.'

'Would it be too much to say you were – are – in love with her?'

'It'd probably be too little.' He flashed his teeth at me; this may have been an expression of amusement. 'I was down bad. She was good about it, though. She didn't mind. But I always got the feeling that she was neither for nor against being with me.'

'What makes you say that? Did you read what you printed out?'

'No. There wasn't any need. I can't understand people who research each other when there's nothing preventing them from talking to each other.'

'I see. And what were you told she wanted from her time with you?'

He ran a hand through his hair, shook water droplets off his fingers and tutted at them. 'A kind of lie detector. She thought that scent could be so disarming that it compels absolute truthfulness.'

'But that isn't what you're interested in?'

'The "real" me or the "real" you? No. But I do think a lot about other parts of that sentence. The "me" part, and the "you" part. I've noticed that a lot of angst festivals I've been on the fringes of get started with a defective understanding of what's entering "our" circumstances from my side and what's entering from your side. There's a third factor, something like a set of performance prompts that don't come from either of us – I don't know where those prompts come from or what they really are, and I don't care about that, actually. I care about not letting the third factor take over.'

'Can you give me an example?'

He could: 'When I was around eighteen, nineteen, I had three close friends . . . you know, the inseparable type. If you only saw one of us, at least two of the others would appear before you could count to ten. All boys, naturally. We didn't talk to girls. Talking to girls was like a ruthless quiz: no correct answers, no prizes and no way to escape having your wrong answers dissected by members of the audience for days. Me and the boys could just say ridiculous shit and forget about it. It was great, though the mood changed a bit when two of us went to one university, our other friend went to a different university and the fourth got a job. Not a legal job, but it was environmentally friendly and . . . he was kind of a rapid thinker, so it was important that he found something that kept him engaged in that way . . .'

'Just say it.'

'He was part of the night shift overseeing a hydroponic marijuana farm.'

'And the rest of you judged him for not going to uni?'

'Judged him?'

'He was so smart . . . he didn't go to uni, but he was really very smart . . . I'm hearing unnecessary defensiveness on his behalf.'

'Oh. Maybe we did judge him. At the time I don't think we were aware of that, but we probably . . . look, I'm telling you about these friends because of what happened to him – to the friend who got a job instead of studying, I mean. He was assaulted. Sexually. He really was, Kinga.'

'Why are you saying it like that? Did you think he was lying at first?'

'No. When he told us I was kind of awed that he'd put what had just happened to him into our hands the way he did. He was like, you're my best friends, I don't want to keep this, I don't want this to feed on me while I try to get out from under it without saying a word, if I can't tell you guys then there's nobody on earth I can tell, and I'm scared that if I don't say anything about what happened, time isn't going to be able to fix anything for me, time is only going to keep pushing me back to what happened. And then we other three dropped our "boys being stupid" stuff and we were like, we've got you. Tell us everything you can.'

'And did he?'

'Yes. Not immediately. Over the course of a few days. We got there sort of by talking almost in a feminine way – around and around the outskirts of some other topic, and then: boom, a direct thought thrown in like a grenade.'

'Sounds like a mixture to me,' I said. 'Feminine strength lies in endurance – it's the masculine strength that's explosive.'

'Oh yeah? And how about what we did when our friend finally managed to tell us everything he could? Three professional clever-clogs working on removing their blue-collar friend's memory of what had happened to him – which direction would you say that leans in?'

'Different axis . . .'

'Right. Our . . . concern for him was spherical that way, wobbling and rolling over and mowing everything down. We just started asking him all these questions, Kinga. We kept modifying what he'd told us until he was no longer sure that he had an accurate understanding of what assault even is . . .'

'And why exactly did you do that? Do you know?'

'From my side, I was trying to fix it. I thought that if he didn't think he'd been raped, then – in a way, he wouldn't have been.'

'And your other two friends? Did they ever say anything about their reasons?'

'No. We could only make it happen while pretending it wasn't happening. But I do think we were all thinking about him. That was the problem – thinking about him, not being right in it along with him, as it had been with most things we'd done or told each other about before. I'd open my mouth to talk to my friend and all this stuff that wasn't us would just jump out and position him in a more comfortable place – or a less painful place. You shouldn't stand by while your friend is in pain, right? You should just stop the pain. That was the gospel according to this thing that wasn't really us and wasn't really him, anyway. He fought us for his memory, but we were *very* firmly evasive, and after a few days of that, he slumped. After a couple of weeks of our fucking shameful tampering, we got our friend to very timidly tell us the new version – that something had happened between him and this woman, and it was something he didn't like, but nothing he couldn't learn from . . . and you could see, as he was saying it, that he knew it wasn't true, but you could also see complete fatigue. He couldn't talk to any of us any more. And after that day, he didn't. He changed his phone number and everything.'

'Good for him.'

'Then . . . the other two may have changed their phone numbers, too – I don't know, because I didn't text or call them again either. I'd go to send them a photo, or a link to something, but we were no longer ourselves, so I'd just end up messaging someone else.'

'Fucking hell, Mr Ngô.'

'We were only at the start of our twenties. He found better friendships, and the rest of us became better friends, I hope. The best way to be a person amongst other people is to say and do things that come from you and perceive the words and deeds that come from them, but it's not as simple as wanting to be that way when there's this third thing that destroys whatever you try to do for each other.'

'You believe that fragrance has the power to delineate.'

'I do.'

'Even if it doesn't, it might be important in other ways. A lot of the time I don't take too much of an interest in what I can smell, other than in a "yes, please" or "no, thank you" way. But scent probably plays some sort of subliminal part in what makes some moments in life feel like more pressure than one person can bear, whilst other moments are pretty much a picnic . . . did I say something funny?'

This time he was more than semi-smiling. 'Sorry. Your message here is that my stamp collection is very nice, you can see it means a lot to me and I must keep it up because it's bound to be worth millions in future. You've chosen to encourage me, and that's kind. But it's strange to hear you saying these things in her voice.'

'I'm sorry.'

'For what?'

'I don't know.'

He looked at the ceiling for a moment, then he said, 'This won't do. Come here.'

I folded my arms across my chest. 'I think I could manage that if I was asked politely.'

'Come here, please, other Kinga.'

I approached his chair, very slowly, walking heel to toe,

waiting for him to say *Stop*. But he said nothing until I was standing right beside him. He swivelled his chair towards me and pointed at his silk-clad thigh. 'Put your foot here.'

'Why?'

'Don't you want to learn how I know that she's gone?'

I raised my foot, lowered it to the ground again, removed a slipper and a sock at his request, and after that, with an awkward hop, I was half standing in his lap. He steadied me with one hand at my ankle and one at my knee, looking up at me, gaze cold, touch colder. But through the sole of my foot I could feel waves of heat building and breaking, racing towards me, past me—

I became aware of him asking if I was OK, so of course I was all 'Never better', etc.

'So,' he said, lightly drumming his fingers against my knee, 'about nine months ago, we agreed on four places to spray the perfume I send her.'

(Her . . . she . . . Kinga-E, you're as nameless to your perfumer as Jarda is to you.)

He asked me to guess the first spot – this was easy. The ankle. Its distance from her nose meant that if something in the latest adaptation of the formula didn't smell good to her, after a single spray she could consider that day's perfume application complete and go about her day without being too disturbed by it.

Apparently, last night Mr Ngô presented her with two versions of the very-nearly-final formula.

'Very-nearly-final?'

He knew that it's our saint's day tomorrow. Between his not being Catholic and the unlikelihood that Kinga-E would bring this up in conversation, he really must've been down bad.

'I wanted it to be ready in time. A personal gift for a personal day, if you will. I just needed her to wear one version last night, and the second version tonight, then I'd make a tweak that has been niggling at me, and that would be it.'

'But now?'

'Now I'm back to square one.' He reached behind me to grab one of the 2ml decants, and he spritzed his wrist before offering it to me to smell. I smelled earth and iron. 'A chest full of coins being buried by moonlight,' I said. He told me to stop flirting with him – 'How many times do I have to say it? I'm spoken for' – and he lowered his nose to my ankle before reporting: 'Cinnamon.'

He sniffed again, drawing delicate and deliberate circles with the tip. Of his nose. Of his nose!

'Cinnamon bomb, actually. On you, this smells like a Christmas cookie with just a touch of something herbal that could've fallen into the mix by accident.'

'It didn't smell like this on her.'

'No.'

'Is . . . er, is cinnamon not present in your formula, then?'

'It is. Tons of the stuff. I'm putting a lavender–cinnamon accord at the heart of this formula. Just a little coarse, and sweet – not a sweetness found in anywhere in nature, but something more thermal, more like a cuddle. Sweet enough to pierce memory. Can a scent affect your senses so strongly that you begin to remember things that haven't yet taken place? That's the type of disturbance the two of us were chasing. You can take your foot down; thank you.'

He stood. The second and third spots were the shoulders. He nuzzled his way along those. That is, if it's possible to nuzzle without touching . . . I don't know, he was explaining the difference between what the formula says to him when I wear it and what it had been saying to him through all these months of trial and error with Kinga-E. He says Kinga-E's skin absorbed cinnamon molecules with a vengeance; he could never get that note to last longer than five minutes on her. He'd responded with a cinnamon overdose. He hadn't been able to let go of this combination, and now I was throwing the excess born of his rigidity right back in his face. He was speaking so softly that it was like being stroked with words or something, and I can't be expected to keep my head in such conditions.

The left ankle had been surveyed, the shoulders had been surveyed . . . the fourth spot was between my breasts. Kinga-E, you told us he kept physical contact with you to a minimum, but every Friday WAS fornication Friday! This perfumer was all over you. You were at it like rabbits – at it every time you sprayed him (alright, the work of his imagination) onto the four places of his choosing. That's a lot of vital fluid, O anointed one.

Special Ks, 'Sacrifice' is this impassioned perfumer's proof that we're not mad – or not merely mad. I'm not sure what to make of that. We may not be able to be in the same place at the same time, but we do share – well, everything else. Our skin is actually the same.

What is perfume, really? How can it switch vocabularies like this?

At the end of every Holy Communion catechism class, Father Wojewoda would always announce that we could ask him anything, anything at all; he'd assure us that there was no such thing as a stupid question. So then we all started gabbling away. And it wasn't a ruse to unveil nominees for excommunication – our parish priest gladly tried his best to address all that curiosity about our faith. I had the same question every week, but never managed to shout WHAT'S UP WITH ALL THE INCENSE AT CHURCH loudly enough to be heard.

I bet Mr Ngô has some theories about the religious use of incense. I could have talked with that man all afternoon. Then again, I rarely meet anybody I can't talk to all afternoon, and could feel that this was anathema to Dr Holý, who used to struggle with the percentage of session time I spent trying to understand him until I got switched to a day outside of his office hours. I'm even more curious about Kinga-E's perfumer, though I really don't like him for Kinga-E, and by extension, for us Special Ks.

Don't read this as me being on some quest for perfection in a partner. I get that everyone's a two-for-one deal: Jekyll + Hyde. But I think you should be able to honestly say 'I'm his friend!' when presented with Jekyll, and the same thing when presented with Hyde, even if one of those affirmations has an unspoken 'I know he's a lot, but . . .' squeezed into the spaces between the words. And the way I find myself watching out for Mr Ngô's spite, I don't think I could ever really feel like I'm on his side, or that he's on mine. Actually, while I'm thinking about this, I'll revise whatever it was I said about finding him beautiful to look at. The further we got into our conversation, the more I realised that my reluctance to take my eyes off Dinh Châu Ngô isn't just about him looking good. I've intuited that he's a person who's capable of saying really awful things. Not by accident, either. He talks like someone whose perception of cruelty is far too lucid for any unintentional attack. And that makes me careful too. With enough vigilance, you can spot the moment when someone is about to take aim and you can strike first.

There had actually been multiple dialogues taking place all along: Mr Ngô and I talked, and through the speakers all around us, the soldiers of *Merry Christmas, Mr Lawrence* were speaking with each other too. The dialogue stopped, music took its place, and I switched my gaze from Mr Ngô to the film projection on the wall. And tears welled up in my eyes. Not from any particular emotion, as far as I can tell – I just didn't want to blink, so I put it off until it hurt not to. I was increasingly . . . if I felt anything, it was something like surprise. Maybe amazed is the word I want. I kept getting more and more amazed by the blurred light and by the gloom that glistened, amazed by the parts of the image that were static and the parts that leaned and swayed as if some gaseous weight was pressing down on them. It was a night scene. I was looking at a man who had been buried alive in sand – but only up to the neck. He wasn't really awake any more, he was permanently dreaming now, all ideas about who or what he was or why any of this had been done to him – all of that was gone. Still, he kept his eyelids open. He looked as if he was waiting for something. Whatever he was waiting for didn't happen, but something else happened: someone ran out of the darkness behind him. An officer with scissors shining in his hand. The officer lifted a few locks of the buried man's hair, cut them, and hurried away, tucking the hair into an inner pocket of his jacket.

If I've understood Mr Ngô correctly, he wants his perfume to reset this scene as a mist someone can walk through on the way to meet friends and foes. A war has screeched and rumbled down to its final days, and it's taken you with it – you're buried up to the neck, but instead of the sand from the film, it's a field of purple flowers. The company of these purple flowers is the final squadron that occupies whatever parts of you are still human, the purple flowers are the last thing you know, and knowing them so very wholly prevents you from making other distinctions . . . you can no longer distinguish yourself from all the injury your being has caused, and all the good you've done just by existing as well.

'I think biographies should begin nine months before the subject is born and end nine months after their life does,' said Mr Ngô. 'Or even continue with notes on the life of a man who couldn't stop himself from claiming a lock of the subject's hair – and the lives of anyone else who comes into possession of that keepsake over the centuries it can last if properly preserved. I don't think we arrive and leave all that suddenly, do you?'

There are two things Mr Ngô said I must be sure to tell Kinga-E, so here they are:

The name of the perfume he's making for you remains the same. 'Sacrifice' is the name his grandma wanted, and Mrs Le is always going to get what she wants if Dinh Châu has anything to do with it. But there's more to it: he thinks that if you and he had been able to watch *Merry Christmas, Mr Lawrence* together, you'd have accepted that he wasn't trying to tempt you into a needlessly cramped position on a pacifist panel. The film would almost certainly have drawn you in to his proposition that lavender and sacrifice are both flowerings so sublime that they shatter death. Listen . . . I was sold on it. Then again, I suppose I ain't so tough.

The other thing . . . I'm told Kinga-E only agreed to regulate those four sprays of perfume in exchange for a piece of information from Mr Ngô. He wrote in his ad that he knows he's found his muse *when, having first encountered that person in a mundane setting, they begin to visit me in my sleep, and befriend me in dreams.* She wanted to know what he dreamed about her.

Kinga-Eliška Sikora, a couple of nights after you first met for coffee, Dinh Châu Ngô dreamed that he robbed a bank with you. It all went well – beginner's luck, maybe – until you reached the bank vault that was meant to set you both up for life. This vault was reputed to contain the nation's most price-less treasure, yet when you got in there, it was crammed full of purple cabbages on long stems ... you know the kind. Decorative cabbages, they're called. In Mr Ngô's dream, he was beside himself. *How are we going to hide all these cabbages?* he asked you. You told him not to fret, you said you knew what to do.

He says he'll tell you the rest next time he sees you.

∷

The screening of *Merry Christmas, Mr Lawrence* came to a close, and that felt like a natural cue to get going, so I asked Mr Ngô if he happened to have seen my phone anywhere.

'I thought you'd never ask me,' quoth he, opening his desk drawer and handing the phone over, along with remarks about me turning out to be from the twenty-first century after all, etc.

It was set to airplane mode. That didn't seem good. I have a few friends who don't use that setting on aeroplanes or during work meetings or the theatre, but do go straight for airplane mode after making a social-media post that they suspect everyone's going to give them shit about. I zipped up my mental hazmat suit as I restored the phone's usual functions. Missed calls and messages from Jas streamed in, interspersed with a couple of messages each from other contacts. Nothing angry or alienating. I double checked for messages from an unknown number – calling our flat to see how Jarda was doing wasn't an option, what with our not having a landline, so he could've texted – but no such messages appeared. I can only conclude that Kinga-E had been very simply, and very dramatically, seeking to enjoy her alone time with Mr Ngô. Huh. I looked at Mr Ngô again – searching, really, for the source of her enthusiasm.

'Everything OK?'

Just as I was answering yes, the situation swerved. The phone began ringing in my hand; Mum was calling. It's always because she's met a new man to live in symbiosis with, or because she can't bear that her daughter is living without that kind of relationship and urgently needs to brainstorm ways and means of making us just like her. Sikora women have to look after men more than they look after themselves. That's how she's decided to conceive of the household she grew up in, and that's what she transmitted to me, putting Dad and Benek first, then, once Benek was both self-sufficient and a star, she moved on to Ziggy, Hakim, Lars and the other stepsomethings who weren't quite fathers but definitely didn't feel like siblings. I know the boyfriends are a hassle for Benek, mostly because no matter how much money Mum's men might already have, they either want to be his new agent or manager or they have business ideas they think he'd be crazy not to invest in. It's very weird . . . our gentle, superlatively loving mother continually exposes her children to people who sort of froth at the mouth trying to control them. I asked her about it once, in those exact words: 'Mum, don't you think it's weird that . . . ?' and she came right back with, 'I guess this is how your fancy therapist is teaching you to think. You know, people used to be able to make normal connections with each other before all of this navel-gazing.' So . . . maybe there was a mix-up at the hospital, maybe the one who actually gave birth to us is out there somewhere completely dumbfounded by the experience of having raised a woman who can't even put her socks on without getting somebody else's opinion first.

'Hi, Mum,' I said, making a 'please wait' gesture in Mr Ngô's direction. 'How are you, and how soon will I be seeing you?'

'Kinga?' She sounded as if she hadn't expected me to pick up . . . has she been calling throughout the week without success? That's our mother, Special Ks . . . don't be so cold. 'Have you been well, darling? With the different personalities? I'm speaking with Kinga-Casimira today, right?'

'Nope, this is Kinga-Eliška.'

'Oh, I'm sorry!' I could hear that she was. Am I the only Special K who actually gets on with Mum? The rest of you only seem to acknowledge her existence grudgingly, if at all. Before the rest of you label me President of her Fan Club: I'm not saying we're close – we can't be, we've never really found meaning in the same places – but we take note of each other. I try to keep track of her as she undergoes her unavoidable trials, and I think she does the same with me. That counts for something.

'No harm done, Mum. Are you in town?'

'Yes! Just for today, you know. Miguel's taking me shopping on Pařížská. Is there anything you want? Just tell me, I can pick up something for you. Oh, wouldn't you like a nice new hat? Not everyone can wear hats with *aplomb*, but you do.'

'A very sweet thought, Mum, but no hats. Can I look forward to seeing you at dinner?'

'Alright, so you're free? It'll be me, you and Duarte. You'll like Duarte. His son's a sportsman, you know – a real dynamo, just moved here to play for, ah, Sparta, is it? Sorry, no – the other one. Slavia . . .'

'Great, well, bring him over.'

'Wouldn't you rather we choose a restaurant? We don't want to impose, and it'd be unfair to make you feel like a third wheel at your own place.'

'A third wheel?' I smiled at Mr Ngô. 'Why would I feel like a third wheel when I, too, am currently pair bonded?'

Mr Ngô looked up from his notebook – he'd been writing something up until then.

Oops. Was I supposed to de-escalate the situation at home? But I'm not one of those Kingas. De-escalation is more in Kinga-A or Kinga-D's line, no? I'm Team Toxic, and I count three of us in total: Kinga-B, Kinga-E and me.

There was a long and very interesting silence after I confirmed that dinner would be a double date. I half thought Mum was going to start shouting 'Hello? Hello?' and make me lie to her again, but she opted for an 'I always knew you could do it' attitude: 'Wonderful! Then we'll see you at seven? Don't buy wine, we'll bring the good stuff. Pa pa!'

'Can't wait, pa pa,' I said to her, then, to Mr Ngô: 'I need your help.'

'I'll do my best,' he said. 'I know I'm not meeting any of your family members tonight, so I'm calm.'

'How did you know that?'

'Well – my first instinct was to ask if you and I are pair

bonded. But if you have to ask, and all that . . .'

I golf-clapped. 'So much more than just a pretty face and a nuanced nose!'

'That's yet to be proven. What do you need?'

'The address of a place where one can shop for a woman who has pretty much everything. Without spending very much money at all. I just know that you know where to go.'

He opened his desk drawer again, took out a business card and put it into my hand. 'For your records.' And he offered to drive me to the address on the card.

Children, we trekked many miles to reach our getaway car. Many miles, I say, across fluffy fields ablush with a colour somewhere between olives and blueberries. It was cold, but he had this nifty pair of heated gloves – the kind you charge via USB – I wore one of the gloves, he wore the other, and he bundled both our ungloved hands up inside his jacket pocket. I wondered what it would be like if Jarda and Mr Ngô were in the same room. I'd really like to be there for such a meeting one day.

Mr Ngô dropped me off at a pawn shop in Kobylisy. From the outside, it looked like a sliver of a thing squashed in between an estate agency and a food bank. Inside: four floors of postponed gladness linked by tiled staircases – all harlequin-patterned, and all squeaky clean. In some ways it felt more like an animal sanctuary than a shop. Everything on display was in such excellent condition that I couldn't quite believe that these items had been brought in looking this good. And each item was showcased in such a way that you could pick it out with ease if that was the only thing you were looking for. It's pure villainy to shop at a place like this, where the prices are so low, and a single impression hovered over every glass case: the objects and their original owners longed to reunite. But there was no way I was leaving that place without a gift. I don't need that to make sense to anybody else, but I know that Benek prepares for first encounters with Mum's men this way too. We wouldn't want her highly attentive yet low-maintenance ways to be seized as permission to treat her like someone who has no choice but to cope with whatever scraps some pair of trousers might throw her. So: her children make the boyfriends watch them presenting tributes. I picked out a rococo-style egg chandelier bestrewn with painted hens in gilded chariots, and I went home to make dinner. I worked a little bit on the tram to offset the cost of what I'd just bought: my income may not be as regular as some, but I blag my way into funds here and there. Years and years ago, when I still used to go out dancing in Vinohrady, I kept meeting very pretty girls who had money, genuine friends, acceptable suitors, projects they cared about, everything they could ever want, except mystique. They could've just been playing some form of femininity Pokémon game (gotta catch every single classic trait) but the way these club contacts of mine went on about wishing they were mysterious made it seem as if that was what they wanted more than anything else. After a few shots and a few BFF pledges, I'd look at all the inspirational sayings my new friends regularly posted online, and I'd suggest a drastic reduction in output. Now, aside from a three- or four-word post a couple of Saturdays per month, they only appear on their followers' feeds when tagged by friends who are hyping them up. The three- or four-word post is written by me, and it's rarely a complete sentence. The posts could be interpreted as drafts finalised too early, or the beginnings of thoughts too deep to be fully expressed, half-hellos from a really, really busy person who still wants to stay in touch, or anything else you're inclined to come up with. Replies and comments to these posts are never deleted, and never read. Not by me, anyway. I hear that people have become friends and/or foes by replying to each other's comments, but that could've been a ploy to get me to read them. The truth is, I'd be nervous to make these kinds of posts from my own account: Czech netizens are far too fucking good at dragging a bullshitter with words alone. These kids know how to make you rue the day you became literate. Having scrolled through many a comment section in my day, I feel confident in saying that only Scots are anywhere near as skilled in the martial art of online commentary. That's why I think the fees I receive are reasonable. These three-to-four-word posts made from somebody else's social-media account provide the benefits of mysteriousness whilst removing the anxiety of it. The secret ingredient is not actually caring how the post comes across, and that always comes at a cost.

I went straight to the fridge as soon as I got home. Burrata, pink tomatoes, balsamic vinegar that's older than we are . . . thanks to Kinga-A, we already have the kind of starter that will put Mum and Duarte at ease. There was basil too – not too wilted, either. I got some bossa nova going while I assembled the food-prep kit – chopping board, knives, etc: 'Siri, play "Waters of March". Actually, start a radio station for "Waters of March".'

The music started, I sang along (in made-up Portuguese that I wanted to get out of my system before Duarte arrived), a tall, long-haired man slid timidly into the room – if I would liken him to anything, it's to the sort of ruddy beige still-life Babcia and Dziadek liked: he's roasted chestnuts and cream in a big brass pitcher. Not at all the rogue Kinga-A described. Not Kinga-E's totally over-the-top adversary, either. He strikes me as a rustic type who's got in over his head with city wheeling and dealing. This afternoon he hung his head and said in a low, hoarse voice: 'Kinga-Filomena, please allow me to apologise for everything that I am and everything that I've done to date.'

Then we both started talking at the same time, and stopping, and saying to each other, 'No, sorry, please finish your sentence—'

Five songs into the 'Waters of March' radio station rota, we established that:

- Ever since yesterday morning, Jarda, devastated at the thought of his week of wonders coming to nothing, had been alternating between refreshing his e-mail inbox and sleeping to make time pass faster.

- The ransom note and photos had been dispatched as he'd wished. 'Oh, I was updated about THAT. But where did you go? Where were you all night?' he asked, giving me lost-puppy eyes. I mean, LOL, Jarda . . . would you have come running straight back if you were Kinga-E?

- He was more than willing to serve as a sous chef pre-dinner and as my boyfriend during dinner, but he drew the line at googling and attempting a Brazilian recipe. He was all *Look, I don't know much, but I don't think you should embarrass your mum with that kind of welcome. How would you feel if you went to somebody else's house and your host refused to serve you anything except some* pierogi *they'd only learned to make an hour ago?*

- Dinner was to be a test, plain and simple. If Mum approves of him, I do not.

    'And if she doesn't?'

    'Then you have my blessing to take this criminal romance of yours as far as you can. As long as you make sure we get our fair share of the proceeds.'

    'She will not approve of me,' he vowed. Special Ks, I don't know what's the matter with me today – for some reason I found that vow almost too cute to be indifferent towards. But I reminded myself that I mustn't be swayed. There do seem to be sides here, and if that's true, then obviously I'm on ours, and not his.

This Jarda of ours 'swears on his life' that there was no tea- or incense-based misconduct yesterday, and says his apology is for exhibiting an ugly side to his temper during the course of Kinga-E's ostentatious airing-out of our flat and scrubbing of surfaces he'd touched, not to mention the bout of scented-candle-lighting and linen-laundering, all while telling him she can 'smell souls' and his 'fucking stinks like some fucking murderous pig's'. He's such easy company, though. He's somehow free of the insecure ego that a lot of liars seem to suffer from. I roasted some parsnips while he made a mushroom sauce. He got Siri to play us Blossom Dearie's greatest hits; we twirled each other around the kitchen as we sang of our refusal to dance. Four magnificent rib-eye steaks from the Real Meat Society were delivered within the hour, and he'd finished searing them when Mum and Duarte rang the doorbell.

As usual, Mum called me her 'one and only' and she held my face in both her hands and then hugged me for a long time. I kept thinking she was taking it as an opportunity to whisper something, but it turned out the embrace itself contained all that she felt like saying. Behind my back, I felt her wagging her finger at Jarda when he said to Duarte: 'So, you came with Kinga's big sister, but when will their Mum arrive? We were expecting her too . . .'

Duarte grumbled that she certainly had an age-reversing effect. She hadn't let him buy her anything on the most expensive street in Central Europe: 'A big man like me, window-shopping, as if I was a boy with empty pockets again . . .'

Duarte's quite the charmer. His powerhouse of a son, Caio, looks almost nothing him. Duarte's on the daintier side of Black Brazilianness, and absolutely other heterosexual men's worst nightmare – the pretty, well-dressed man your girlfriend spends a lot of time giggling with and tells you not to worry about. He said all the right things about Mum's new egg chandelier, too, declaring that they'll be raising quails at his home in Fortaleza so as to be able to decorate the kitchen properly. There's no telling if he's someone who's really going to go the distance with Mum, but I like the way they look at each other. They're pals. He asks her what she thinks and what she likes, doesn't answer for her, and doesn't appear to be flustered (or pleased) when the novelty of this forces her to investigate her thoughts.

Jarda's efforts to win the disapproval of our dinner guests included helping himself to more beer without asking Duarte if he wanted any, solicitously asking 'Are you sure you haven't had enough?' when Duarte said he wouldn't mind another beer as well, heavily implying that he'd had his feet up scrolling TikTok while I cooked, and asking both Mum and Duarte to consider investing in his fledgling start-up.

'Well, what is it?' Duarte asked, making very obvious effort not to look Mum's way.

'Phone booths. We're bringing phone booths back. But they're sound-proofed, so you can stand in there talking on your mobile without being heard by anyone outside.'

'Mmmm,' said Duarte, and drank more beer.

'You could rent them out on Airbnb as well,' Mum suggested. 'I mean, just for a few hours, so people could take naps.'

She and Jarda looked at each other very seriously for ages. Meanwhile, Duarte had locked eyes with me in exactly the same manner. I stopped myself from laughing by telling myself that if I laughed, Mum was going to show approval of Jarda.

Stony, stony faces, until Duarte relaxed his very slightly: 'Do you mind me asking how you met?'

'Not at all,' Jarda said. 'It was at a ski resort in the Tatras.'

'You learned to ski?' That was Mum. 'This is perfect . . . we can all go together, the six of us.'

'Six . . . ?' Jarda asked.

'Oh yes. Freddie, Kinga's brother-in-law, is a keen skier too. This is going to be—'

'Excuse me,' Jarda said, standing up very quickly, his expression see-sawing. It was clear he was about to break. 'Sorry, I'll just—'

He all but sprinted out of the room, and we heard him having what sounded like a choking fit in the bathroom: he may have stuffed a towel in his mouth.

Duarte started telling me about a nephew of his who was around my age: 'You know, Kinga, it's already been two years since his divorce, I really think he's healed. He runs a whisky distillery, he's a great patron of the arts, he's in good shape . . .'

But Mum placed her hand over Duarte's until he stopped extolling his nephew's virtues. 'Duarte, stop,' she said. 'I think Jarda will do very nicely.'

So there you have it, Special Ks. Mother approves.

Fuck it; Jarda has my blessing all the same.

SUNDAY

3 March 2024
(FEAST DAY OF ST CUNIGUNDE)

Right . . . here I am, Kingettes. Your weakest link, the one who got relegated to Sunday for compulsory bed rest of indefinite duration. You never liked my curiosity about you, you find it creepy. There've probably been times when I've struck you as stalker-on-the-verge-of-penalising-rejection-with-violence creepy. So you've kept me out of your way. And most of you found it all too easy to buy some variation of the hypothesis that I bear murderous contempt for you all.

I'm laughing. Bitterly, but still . . . no, I get it. My approach to keeping up with your news is too insistent, too intent. I compile whatever relevant information I can get hold of, and then I compile some more, even though none of it ever seems to add up to knowledge. I just don't know what else to do. All my faltering compliments on your selfies do is cause you to draw back, or even flee. I've all but strained my eyes poring over the exchanges between Kinga-Casimira and her friend Berenika. Then, in her diary entry for this week, Kinga-C replicates an exchange between them, and – the shock of comprehension knocked me flat for a full minute. Take a look at our phone: you'll see that every single text message between Kinga-C and her bestie is composed solely of emojis. What the fuck is somebody outside of Berenika and Kinga-C's history of in-person banter supposed to do with that? Banjo emoji, bowl of soup emoji, tree emoji followed by a trio of emojis with sunglasses on, and then a fist emoji. What? But now Kinga-C, seeing this coded speech as so very normal that it isn't worth mentioning, suddenly and simply tells us what it all means. It turns out that hardly any of the possible translations I've pondered actually apply.

I also have something to say about Kinga-E's perfumer. Kinga-F seems quite invested in making us dread him, so I want to add a counterbalance from my side. I was only really curious about one thing: I kept thinking someone was going to ask him, but nobody did.

So I called him.

'Hi,' I said, when he finally picked up the phone. 'What did you dream?'

'Hi. Do you mean . . . last night?'

'No. When you advertised for a muse, didn't you write that in some sense you allow your subconscious to decide who the muse will be?'

'Oh. Yes, I wrote that.'

'And was it bullshit, or did you really dream something? If you did, were there two dreams? One for each of your top two candidates?'

'You're nosy,' he observed.

'Does this mean you're not going to tell me?'

'No, I will.'

Dinh Châu told me he dreamed that he and Kinga-Eliška robbed the headquarters of the Czech National Bank. Their ransacking priority was a vault that contained (according to credible sources) the 'nation's most precious treasure'. But the door swung open to reveal bundles of purple cabbage. They rummaged around for something with higher market value, but that was it, just purple cabbage heads on long green stems. The kind you could make floral arrangements with. They had to make their getaway sharpish, so they grabbed a pram each – big prams, the kind with enough room for four babies to recline in comfort – filled them with cabbages and ran for it. They weren't pursued, and nobody at the bank seemed that bothered about the emptying of the bank vault – one employ-ee even said: 'Those cabbages will be back when they're good and ready. They always are.'

Dinh Châu and Kinga-E tried offering the vegetal treas-ure to passers-by, but the passers-by kept claiming that they already had some at home. Eventually Kinga-E checked her watch and said it couldn't be helped, the cabbages would have to come to the Czechia and Slovakia's Got Talent Open Audition at the O2 Arena. Her post-robbery plan had been to audition alone. Startled, Dinh Châu asked Kinga-E what talent she intended to show off, and she said she didn't know – there was bound to be something that showed up at crunch time. And maybe this surplus cabbage fiasco was for the best, maybe the cabbages needed to be put under a bit of pressure before they showed their true mettle.

The hapless robbers wheeled their prams up to the great silvery disc in the west and joined the queue that snaked all the way across the two neighbouring districts. As they waited, they counted their cabbages and filled out an application form for each one.

'And? What happened when you got to the front of the queue?'

'Oh, I woke up before that happened.' He says what he mostly recalls about the Kinga-E in his dream was that once she put her mind to it, she saw such beautiful gifts in each one of those stolen cabbages. There was no conjecture involved; she saw all these attributes clearly; she *knew* them. The Kinga-E in Dinh Châu's dream picked up cabbage after cabbage, looked at it closely, then turned to him and said with the utmost seriousness: *Here's Bazyli: he can defuse a bomb in under nine seconds. Quick, write that down. Nobody's ever seen cabbage do that, have they? And this one, Thùy Sang, she plays Chopin's piano concerto with her toes, much more soulfully than most virtuosos play with their fingers.* There was another one called Radim who was an archery whiz, and it struck D.C. that filling out those forms on behalf of those cabbages was more of a marvel to him than the auditions themselves could ever be. Then came the cruel and classic dig that only dreams can deliver: there was only one form left, and Kinga-E said, Dinh Châu, it's time to talk about your talents. He wrote his name and waited to hear what claim to make, Kinga-E started telling him, and it was the most wonderful and most unexpected thing, and then he was awake and it was all gone.

'Huh,' I said. 'And what about the dream that had Kinga-E's friend in?'

'A completely different dream. You want to hear about that too?'

'Yes, I do.'

'Tough,' he said, and hung up.

I tried to call Dr Holý, but it looks like he's changed his number. Sorry about that, Kinga-D. It probably wasn't meant to be anyway.

We all know that this boy-chasing was procrastination to take the focus off the situation I'd got us into. Since 7 a.m., Jarda had been knocking on the bedroom door at intervals, and I'd been telling him that I felt sick and asking him to come back in five minutes. At around 10 a.m. he said that I couldn't be all that sick if I was chatting away and giggling girlishly on the phone, and he commanded me to 'open up RIGHT NOW'. I did, and he was standing there with a platter of hard-boiled eggs arranged into a pyramid (he'd skewered them five at a time – could they really have been in the fridge all along? That many eggs?) so that's what he had in one hand: the egg pyramid. In the other he had a candle on a candlestick. He took a deep breath and started singing 'Happy svátek to you, happy svátek to you', walking backwards because I headed straight for him in order to move the festivities to the sitting room.

He continued singing until I blew out the candle, then he handed me the egg pyramid and flopped down onto the sofa, gesturing for me to help myself to some eggs. 'You've got to, on your saint's day,' he said. 'It's bad luck if you don't.'

'Really? Where did you hear that?'

He steepled his fingers under his chin.

'That's not the main question to be asking right now.'

'Then what is?'

This is what he asked me: *How come it's Sunday again?*

I took an egg off a skewer and stared at him as I pulled the shell away. He stared back, somewhat goatishly. (Something about the way he pushes his chin forward. Something about the way his gaze flickers, too.)

He didn't add anything to his question, so it was up to me: 'Do you mean that you've lost a week?'

'I mean that all I remember is coming over on Sunday evening, one thing leading to another, you tying me up and saying you'd be right back, and then NOT FUCKING COM-ING BACK . . . why do you do that? Are you one of those "out of sight, out of mind" people? Whatever makes you like that, it's not OK . . . I may or may not have fallen asleep shouting your name as loudly as the gag let me. And then next thing I know, I'm waking up at sunrise on your sofa.'

I cracked a second egg shell and peeled it off, looking deep into his eyes as I did so. Then I offered Jarda the egg. He took it and ate it whole.

'I think you're lying,' I said. 'I think you remember everything.'

I'm the one who promised to help him. He told me he need-ed to hide, and I told him we'd hide him for the week. At some point during day one, my friend's political instincts must have kicked in. He must have worked out that I'm the Kinga with the lowest standing, my word wouldn't be enough to secure his stay, and he'd have to keep us unnerved and unsure as to the right thing to do. That's what I think, though Jarda unequivocally denies this. You try asking him, and don't let him off until he slips up.

Kingettes, this story begins in April 2023. You know our neighbour, Aleš? Thin, balding guy, kind of a community spirit in a way that leaves you ambivalent? It was nice that he hosted weekly gatherings for the Ukrainian refugees who came to stay with him and a bunch of our neighbours, but the atmosphere was a bit . . . I mean, it felt like he was hostile towards anyone who didn't seem to be in utter despair? Sometimes people laughed as they were telling each other (or being told) tales of the week gone by, and Aleš would glare until the laugher turned their outburst into a cough. I know you're not supposed to say things like this nowadays, so just between us: these vegetarians always overdo it with the morality . . .

Aleš has replaced the tasty comforts of sirloin and pork shoulder with the resolve to make others feel 'at home'. In my case, he falls over himself to mention some Polish superstar every time we run into each other. 'Oh, I watched this Agnieszka Holland film, last night,' he'll purr. 'You must know the one . . .' or 'Wow, I was just thinking about a line from Czesław Miłosz's *The Captive Mind*, and here you are . . .' The guy's heart is in the right place and all that, but my God, should you really have to do that much cultural prep in order to be able to have a chat with someone?

On the first Sunday in April Aleš knocked on our door and asked if I'd be up for leading a shopping trip for a group of pensioners who lived in the same retirement home in Hradec Králové.

'Me? But why . . . I'm not qualified . . . I don't have experience with . . . but why me?' I mumbled, still very much in the 'only fit to stay at home with the curtains tightly drawn' frame of mind the rest of you had assigned me. But Aleš was patient.

'They're just a skip and a hop away from Poland,' he explained. 'Mum and her friends like to cross the border for bargains and adventure, but they've been getting a bit frustrated because even though the food is quite a bit cheaper and the quality is better, their sixth sense for deals keeps telling them they're still missing out. But you know all the secret spots, right?'

Right, Aleš, right, everything to do with Poland is my department . . .

'Oh, I can get them discounts,' I said. 'By asking in Polish.'

'Really?' Aleš narrowed his eyes. 'I knew it! I fucking knew it. As soon as they hear Czech they hide the tofu, too, and say they've never heard of it.'

He coughed up a few more kernels of unfounded paranoia as to all the methods They employed to keep Central Europe dependent on meat, then we got down to business. Aleš agreed to pay me 8,000 crowns to pick a group of twelve up from their fancy dormitory, take them on a grocery-shopping spree and have them back home in time for a late-afternoon nap. The 8,000 was enough to make it worth my while to hire a car, drive up to Hradec at dawn and drive back here at sunset, the home would lend me their minibus for the trip across the border, and I assured him the group would save at least three times as much as he was paying me. He told me his mum couldn't wait to meet me: he said he'd told her a lot about me. A lot? A couple of weeks later, as I assisted former secondary-school headteacher Mrs Beránková in her quest to lift up a wheel of cheese fit for a titan so she could check the underside of it, I asked her what her son had told her about me. It was all just as I'd expected: 'He said you're . . . you know, foreign,' she said. 'And that you're nice, and shy. That's it. Why? Is there anything else I should know?'

Everybody in my shopping group was spryer and more inquisitive than I was: this seemed to be part of the basis on which their clique was formed – the Myers–Briggs Type Indicator had deemed them all extroverts. The buzz I got from these grocery runs, or maybe just from the company of these deli connoisseurs who loved giving and receiving compliments . . . it got to my head. The banter, the singalongs as we puttered down country lanes together, the look of satisfaction on everybody's faces as they hugged their net bags to their chests and whispered: 'This is it . . . this is as cheap as it gets,' all of this made me feel like more than a feeble stub persona that exists to give people chances to do or say 'the right thing'. To help with navigation and general comms stuff I didn't want the rest of you to know about, I bought a second-hand Nokia handset and stashed it in a shoebox all of you avoid because it's full of the unopened letters I've sent to Dad in prison over the years.

I took the Hradec crew shopping again in June, August

and December. It was in December that the voluptuous and fulsome-browed Růžena Ha, commonly acknowledged party girl of the group, pulled me aside in the bakery section of a hypermarket and said: 'Hey, wanna have some fun?'

I said, 'Oh, definitely!' but I honestly didn't know; as soon as I heard the word 'fun' I broke out into a nervous sweat. Růžena administered a few reassuring shoulder-pats. 'It's OK, Kinga-Genovéva, we'll be with you.' She wanted to hitch a ride to Prague with me along with her boyfriend and her cousin. After that I could leave the rest to them; there was this club they'd heard about . . .

Which is how I ended up a worshipper at The Body Temple in Malá Strana. Sounds a bit more like a gym than what it actually is (a strip club), doesn't it? The vaguely athletic name might be part of the system that allows this business to oper-ate on church-owned property that's almost directly opposite the church Kinga-A thinks I so devoutly attend. GPS is fuzzy like that. It's an entirely different kind of communion I partake in across the street. It isn't easy to get in. Which is probably part of what allows the dancers to strip with impu-nity. The entrance corridor is like one of those immortal aids to Habsburg plots and counterplots, the trick cabinets we've seen at museums in Vienna and Innsbruck – full of rattling hollows and handles that don't function. There's a passage-way with several false doorways and a real one, then another, then you have to go down a slide. You've got to wonder what organisation/s this building has been a base for in previous decades. Getting in calls for a blend of concentration and confidence, but getting out is as simple as leaning on the nearest wall . . . multiple doors eject you onto the street quicker than you can say 'bye'. This can't have been a Secret Police venue, then. These are the speculations of a Kingette who sits at the club bar without a drop of alcohol in her. The crowd sounds are a stimulant I don't want to break links with. Plus someone's got to keep a clear head and make sure that the ever-increasing audience of horny pensioners don't get taken advantage of. Not that the dancers are predators – they're just like me in that they're Praguers by way of somewhere else: Ürümqi, Bogotá, Appalachia, Garoua, Cádiz, Uttar Pradesh, Liverpool. Have I been able to exchange sentiments of solidarity with any of them? Not just yet. I'm tongue-tied in their presence, despite knowing all their names and the exact meals each one wolfs down at the end of their shift. Soon enough, the rest of you will meet the Body Boyz too; you'll probably be brave enough to introduce yourself, even, or actually say something when they say 'hi' to you or thank you for picking up their food order. Insofar as any of them expect a verbal reply, or notice that they haven't received one, some of these overwhelming presences seem amused by the silence that tends to fall around them; others are resigned to it or bored by it. The rest look defeated; you can see them deciding that their broken Czech is unintelligible. I don't feel good about contributing to such an illusion, but I've been trying to make up for it by watching them avidly (yes, I know. I really am the creepiest Kingette of all). But actually I contribute less than two per cent of the staring action in that club. When the Body Boyz are onstage, at least a hundred pairs of eyes all stare as one.

It's difficult to describe the effect of these Sunday stripteases. I would say, yes, they're arousing, but they're pitched closer to the aggravating, perturbing bank of that river than the sexually gratifying one. The uniforms belong to priests, monks and altar boys; once all the clothing has finally come off, the bartender pauses bar service and swings an incense censer around so as to drape the visual endgame in one more veil of sweet delay. The finale showers the whole room with virility – ladies and gentlemen swoon all around me – but I'm just sitting there bone dry. Hard to tell if this inhibition is mostly upbringing, or if it's the proximity of an actual church . . .

A typical Sunday scene: I bob my head to Sam Smith's 'Unholy' as Edgar, wearing only a clerical collar and a thong, drops to his knees with a look of absolutely ungovernable naughtiness in his eyes and slinks towards an enraptured grandfather of seven. I shriek along with a few other envious onlookers and try to allow the moment of temptation to pulse through me unimpeded, but I keep thinking we're going to get caught, God is going to send a messenger down here to deliver his verdict upon us. Mark my words . . . unless we change the bar's concept, one of these days an innocent Mass celebrant is going to battle their way into this fortress to ask about gym membership or something, get an eyeful of the Boyz jiggling their perfect bums and suffer some sort of permanent psychotic break. That'll be on our heads and nobody else's.

Even when, at the end of an evening at The Body Temple, I

check in with my libido at home, I have to let go of what I saw at the club. I tried to break the barrier by pushing the wrongness even further, running through verses my imaginary exorcist could pant as he fucks the devil out of me. (Embarrassing as it is, Kinga-A came across one of my attempted selections: that 'seven spirits' verse.) None of it worked. The thought of a blasphemous orgasm is too stressful. I can only come calmly, and these days I come a lot, with soft layers underneath me, without any material covering me, without words, without images, only touch: flick, stroke, clench, rub, ripple. The Body Temple has shown me climactic paths I hadn't sensed the existence of. Without that place, and its Boyz, and its devotees, I don't think any of these good times would have rolled my way.

I've said I don't believe what Jarda said about losing a week, but in fact I don't believe that I don't believe him. There's some way in which I'm open to him, or he to me, that could mean he is the Jarda who gets tucked away until Sunday, and that wherever we go for the rest of the week, we're there together, and are a comfort to each other.

'I'm not going to be here much longer' was one of the first things he said to me, and I replied along the lines of 'Be not discouraged . . .' I'd asked his name, and instead of saying it aloud, he pushed some documents my way with his foot. Judicial summons, shareholder certificates, ratified executive employment contracts, all with his name on them somewhere. Before The Body Temple he'd acted as nominal management for a thoroughbred-racehorse stable, a cinema, one of those pirate-coded sweet shops and then a boxing gym, where he'd got buff and learned that looking the part mitigated some of his subordinates' anger at having to organise everything he was supposed to know how to do. He was not living as a person in his own right, but as some words legitimate enough to be funnelled between loss-generating acquisitions and court disputes. Words and a face when a face is required – that's Jarda. He appears wherever it isn't convenient for his step-father to be seen. He's been (unsuccessfully) charged with involvement in more crimes than we've had hot dinners. The charges are neck-and-neck with the corporate accolades. His talk of 'not being here for much longer' sounded much more ominous than he'd meant it to – next month he'll be sent to run a Christmas-tree farm in Olomouc. His proposition to give the place a bit more multi-season appeal by offering East-er-egg hunts for kids in the spring has already been nixed: the real management says they don't want to deal with that kind of health-and-safety nightmare. An employee called Jarda up and said, 'Respectfully, sir, all we ask of you is that you keep all your ideas to yourself. That's all you have to do in order to be very handsomely rewarded.' Jarda Šimek is in a long-distance relationship with his own life. What more could I want in a close friend? I mean, of course we fucking bonded. Of course we confided in each other! All the kinds of things I've never discussed with you (and vice versa) went straight to that man, and you'd better not harm a hair on his head.

The first four times I visited The Body Temple, I didn't catch so much as a glimpse of him. Perhaps if I hadn't been nosy, we'd never have met at all. On my fifth visit to the club, having

227

wandered away during a performance interval, I decided to slink around the building opening doors, just for fun, and found myself standing in the entrance of a cloakroom lined with trench coats and heavy motorcycle jackets. I wish I could bottle the smell of that room, for Kinga-E, and for me. Somehow it's the smell of forms changing, secretions that are maybe more natural than humans are. The crystallisation of carbon must give off an aroma like this . . .

Jarda was jogging in circles around this cave of night diamonds with a baby over his shoulder. The baby was fast asleep, and when Jarda saw me, he hissed that I should either come in and shut the door or shut the door and leave: 'But whatever you do, it can't be loud . . .'

I spent the next few hours with Jarda and the baby he was minding because one of the Boyz was having childcare issues. Patrice, son of Abdoulaye, would only consent to sleep when in motion; he slept shallowly and screamed with unhinged horror when woken. That's how Jarda and I ended up jogging the evening away, talking quietly as we passed little Patrice between us, extending his nap. The baby showed us as much generosity as he could . . . he didn't mind if we talked. You just couldn't stand still: that was the only thing Abdoulaye's son would make you pay dearly for.

Before I left, Jarda showed me three palpably mid-price-range suits and asked which one made him look most like an asset to society. He had to go to court the next day. I disappointed him by saying that any one of the three would do the trick. Attractive, unattractive, assertive, reactive, I can't assess him for any of those traits. We never once chatted each other up: we were immediately past all that. Jarda told me the direst of dad jokes, kept my glass topped up with sparkling mineral water, and nobody called him boss. Nor did he receive any other tokens of deference. He was right there, but staff would walk up to me and ask me to sign off on admin matters, or I'd be called upon to answer customer queries. He left it all to me: in some sense he hid behind me. Really that was all my friend cared about, hiding – coming across some fold or some corner of this world that could keep him covered and make a secret of him.

It's possible that I just haven't asked him the right questions, but this life goal of Jarda's has never seemed connected to a need to hide from some specific person or thing. Interesting stuff for a hidden persona like me. That which is hidden accrues value: Jarda's convinced of it. If there was anything that would make him happier than being hidden, it would be discovering who wanted him found, and at what expense. That curiosity sounds more materialist than it is: especially since the guy's gone and demanded a ransom off his stepfather.

Jarda's mother, Milica J, whom I enjoy in homeopathic doses, hands me a business card every time she visits the bar. The cards are halo-patterned squares of washi (pale grey paper, gold halos) with the words

Kinga Sikora
General Manager
THE BODY TEMPLE

229

printed on them, along with the address and telephone number. This establishment is only barely legitimate; being our father's daughter, I've frequented enough money-laundering fronts to feel certain that The Body Temple is affiliated with the Luxury Enamel Posse or some other criminal entity. (Kinga-F, burn these pages once the diary gets back around to you. Even though I've made these statements without an atom of proof, we can't be too careful.) But I don't care what The Body Temple 'really' is ... if the job offer was for Sundays only, I'd have agreed already. But she requires a lot more flexibility than that. The Temple itself deserves more, really.

I told Milica this, and she agreed, and laid on some sweet talk:

'And I know you're just what's needed here. Come on, Kinga, you can see Jarda's no entrepreneur; tell me your ideas, all these months I've had my eye on you, and now I'm ready to listen, too. You want to change the name of this place? I'm all ears. The costumes, the music? Just say. I'm tired of training up Body Temple managers only to find that I've let another fucking cuckoo into my financial nest. And I can tell it isn't just about the money for you, you really want to serve up something red hot ...'

Will any of us meet Milica Janković and think 'what's the fuss, there's nothing overwhelming about this lady', I wonder? Personally, it feels like M.J. always comes at me from around a corner, flaring up so fast and bright that there isn't even a fraction of a second to put up my guard; she's already at my throat like some kind of ninja star. For a moment in time, she seemed like a humble person. That's how she caught my attention in the first place. One evening, weeks before I stumbled upon Jarda, Madame took a tray of drinks and nibbles from a waiter and began serving customers herself, asking everybody if there was anything she could do for them and then telling them off when they made suggestions. Růžena Ha was having none of that, and I was sort of hovering in case of who knows what, and right in the middle of her diatribe against 'rural hussies who think they're above it all', Milica suddenly looked over at yours truly, said, 'You're pretty. Just don't expect special treatment,' and then went straight back to insulting Růžena's hairdresser.

Later in the evening, this conviviality-slaying master of ceremonies introduced herself properly, we quizzed each other with example questions from the Czech Life and Institutions Practice Exam database. But Milica's real questions were these: 'Are you reliable? Can I trust you?'

She stared into my eyes and gripped my hands so hard that her diamond rings etched patterns onto my skin.

I stalled; she seemed like the type of drunk who doesn't mind if you stall. 'What about you? Can you be trusted?'

But she did mind: 'EXCUSE ME, I asked first! And if you don't answer me' – she hiccuped – 'there'll be trouble!'

I suggested that bullying was counterproductive. She closed her eyes and shook her head as if listening to her favourite part of her favourite song: 'Pffft, you're only saying that because you've never tried it.'

In short, Milica J is a fundamentally mistrustful person

who sits in the back office of The Body Temple triple-counting the banknotes that are handed to her before she lets the bearer of the envelope leave. She's also a person who's decided she wants to trust someone. And she seems to have zeroed in on me as practice. I could theorise that it's because I'm a new citizen, just like her. But really, as with most fixations, I think it's just that she was around, and I happened to be there too.

Some of the things she says sort of besiege me hours after Milica's gone her way and I've gone mine.

Specifically:

'I've seen what I've seen . . . old patterns are repeating . . .'

'Let's work together and share our abilities while we can. My husband says I sound a bit paranoid when I go on like this, but what do *you* say?'

That kind of thing.

I tell her I don't think it hurts to, you know, have a few preparations in place, and she's all *Sikora, you're a girl after my paranoiac heart.*

If hiding is Jarda's favourite topic, resistance is Milica's. She keeps telling me that 'us difficult newcomers' are here to back up the ones who've always been here to thwart the invaders. And then I go: 'The invaders? What . . . Milica . . . that's history . . .'

And she tells me: 'Not at all, Kinga. Can't you see it's all still in the works? That absolutist lot never give up; they only take breaks. Before long they'll return to the very territories they were chased out of. Gang members and other deviants are the only ones whose principles they've never been able to twist, so

232

all these conflict-averse innocents we're surrounded with are really going to need us when the time comes.'

'When the time comes? You're saying . . .'

'I'm saying – look, there's no sugar-coating this . . . we'll be at war soon. And when you look at what we've got ahead of us, matchmaking is pointless. Sorry, jako.'

'Matchmaking? Why are you bringing that up all of a sudden?'

She waved a hand. 'Just thinking about jobs that should be obsolete already. Anyway: our next war. They'll send the men first, we'll keep the home front going for a while, and then we'll have to pick up other weapons. Every single one we have. And judging by your expression you're maybe doing a bit of statistical work, eh, Kinga? Noticing your poor track record in the field of seeing big trouble coming?'

'Well,' I said, trying to stay calm and mostly succeeding. 'Some people just have a few more blind spots than others, OK? So . . . these auxiliary duties that may or may not be ahead. How soon?'

'Any fucking minute now.'

Listen: I hope with all my heart that this chat is nothing more than Milica's way of glamourising any (unproven!) disregard she may have for the law. All I know for sure is that I promised Jarda I'd hide him for a week in exchange for the ultimate saint's-day gift: a private, one hundred per cent secular-themed performance from the Body Boyz, recorded in our living room by yours truly, for your viewing pleasure. Foolish sympathies aside, I've done what I've done out of a desire to finally share some good times with you, make my own mark on our week for a change, throw a surprise party that would put a smile on all your faces – yeah, I think that completes the list. That's all I wanted, I swear.

I mean, whenever the day OG Kinga was born comes around none of us really seem to consider it our birthday, do we? So why not repurpose our saint's day? Our first birthday as Czech citizens, too – I felt like it was up to me to make today indelible.

Well, the Body Boyz left about an hour ago: yes, it was a sex explosion entirely choreographed by the Boyz themselves, and yes, you'll find the recording on our desktop . . . the file name is BIRTHDAY BOMB, and under no circumstances will I forgive its deletion. This was the big bang I had planned for us, not a St Cunigunde's Day Massacre.

But first, Jarda and I had a ransom to go and wait around for. The handover point was in Divoká Šárka, by a footbridge that passed through a linden copse and ended at the foot of this ancient-looking wooden mill that was said to be under a water goblin's protection because it hadn't yet burned down despite close proximity to near-perpetual barbecues. This was the part we both dreaded, a kind of fusion of our experience as the offspring of father figures who were indifferent to us but thought the sun shone out of our sibling's arse. We were off to the water goblin's mill to get confirmation that the photos and ransom note had been ignored. Jarda switched his phone on, scanned a few of the group chats he was in, answered a few opinion polls on topics he covered with his other hand.

Charming. We're meant to be in this together . . .

We walked to the underground car park where Jarda had left his car, and I put a balaclava on while he drove. Daddy may not care enough to pay up (or send anybody to Jarda's rescue) but he might care enough to ambush the kidnapper who had the audacity to ask for money. It was a hopeful hint at action, just something to raise our spirits. I was dreading the change this would bring about in him, the lessening of life force. It was like taking my soul to the dentist. He would have this terrible look on his face but he'd keep saying 'As expected', and 'It's fine, at least now I know'. This man, the only other person I've ever met with less ambition than me, had hidden for a whole week, and not been found, not even by us. But I honestly don't think there's any more we could have done for him. It's really unfair if he really did lose the week; it means he didn't even get to enjoy a week off work.

It was cloudy today, and the trees were full of tattered buds that had leaped for the light too early; I tried not to look, but they were everywhere, bright half-lives crawling along the shadowy branches.

'Maybe we should have blackmailed him instead,' I said.

He gave an irritable shrug. 'We've already been over and over that . . . I know how he deals with blackmail: big-time loss of temper, he doesn't even hesitate, he'd make us disappear for real.'

'Right, you did say. I still think you being the son of the woman he loves probably counts for something.'

'Whatever,' he said, flatly. 'I guess we'll never know.'

We'd only been standing hand-in-hand by the watermill for around two minutes, me and Jarda, each of us silently recording this encounter with apathy – the sullen stare of the sky, the water in the creek babbling daddy-doesn't-care-daddy-doesn't-care as it washed pebbles down to the valley – there were only two minutes of that, and then darkness zigzagged in front of our eyes; forcing the commotion to take definite shape, I saw – made myself see – that it was a troupe of long oval bundles attached to silk parachutes. The bundles settled silently on the bridge, and then they rose to their feet, and the wooden planks groaned under the weight of their marching. I don't know why Jarda didn't run, but for my part, fight-or-flight mode made a half-hearted attempt to activate but immediately understood itself to be meaningless in this context. Entranced by the steady footfall, I was having thoughts like: *Huh, so unhurried, these are creatures that know time is their ally and not mine.* Things got better for a minute or two – the sound of the marching receded a little; the parachutists had decided to go the other way, deeper into the woods – but then we heard swearing, and some camouflaged figures clad in boiler suits sprang out of the bushes, picked up the bundles, turned them around and gave them little pushes to get them going back in our direction. At that Jarda and I both lost our minds – I mean, what were these objects, little robots bearing explosive devices, what? As soon as we saw humans to aim at, we delved into our pockets – thus discovering that both of us had stashed away hard-boiled eggs of last resort as we were leaving the flat – and threw our own missiles as hard as we could, pushing each other back and shouting 'Go, GO!'

The eggs didn't hit anything but grass, so all in all there was no holding back the steady wave of . . . tortoises. Instead of fleeing, the tortoise-wranglers picked up the stray eggs and threw them back at us. Their aim was far more accurate than ours had been. Afterwards, these semi-sinister figures stood with their hands on their hips, making certain that none of the tortoises turned back. And they shouted about not moving a muscle if we knew what was good for us: *You'd just better fucking not, that's all!*

Gasping, covered in fluffy clods of protein, Jarda and I awaited our fate.

Which took its sweet time crinkling our way. My vision blurred and then sharpened and blurred again; I think Jarda's must have done the same, because we kept saying to each other: 'Can you . . . is that . . . are they?' until the four-legged parachutists were close enough for it to be irrefutable that each one was carrying a bundle of five-thousand-crown notes on his or her back . . . hundreds of tiny portraits of Czecho-slovakia's Founding Father peering up at us, his grave and temperate gaze only slightly obstructed by the carefully tied ribbons that kept him in place. Daddy does care. He cares big time. The leader of the tortoise troupe stopped right at my feet and nosed a nearby egg, which Jarda hurried to de-shell with shaking hands and muttered admonitions: 'Careful now – don't choke,' that sort of thing. So I considered the envelope on top of the first stack of cash mine to open. There was a photocopy of our ransom note inside it, red-stamped with the word PAID, with a condition added in a hasty scrawl of indigo ink (busy stepfather being busy):

Additional supplement of a month's wages added, as
K. Sikora is to report to work at The Body Temple from
4 March 2024.

Here's our current standing, Kingettes: I could say no. Saying yes means we'd really be reporting to two bosses: Milica and this fellow who issues his curt commands in blue purple. Contradictory orders, loyalty tests, the juggling of whims, all this and more will be ours to figure out throughout the work week. You – we – can say no. We can always do that. But think some more: what would we be refusing, really? The need to hash out a different, fairer rotation, with each of us getting weeks or months or even seasons rather than hurrying to do all our living in a day? No to finding more common ground, no to mutual friends and mutual foes? No to trying our luck with all seven of our coins in one go? Back me up, please, Kingettes. I promise to be firm about our time off.

All in favour of transforming The Body Temple, say aye. No more mud-slinging, please, no more hurling of thunderbolts. Don't wait to drop in a snide remark on the day of the week we agreed was yours during the previous regime. I've kept this entry as short as I could so that each of you can read it all now and answer before midnight. One more thing: Jarda's gone home, so don't even think of taking this chance to run out and smooch with him or harangue him or whatever you might feel like doing.

Once again: All in favour of our new new Kinga, say aye.

I'll go first.

AYE.

                                                        Sigh. Aye.

AYYEEEEE   . . . Aye . . .

Aye, but you don't get to choose our birthday, Kinga-Genovéva, we're coming back to this later—

                                                              Aye!

Yes, fine

Prague, Czechia

1 August 2022 to 27 January 2024

ACKNOWLEDGEMENTS

Thank you, Tracy Bohan, thank you, Professor Cieplak, thank you, Petr Onufer, thank you, Jin Auh, thank you, Louisa Joyner, thank you, Sarah McGrath, thank you, Jordaine Kehinde, and Meredith Pal – thank you.

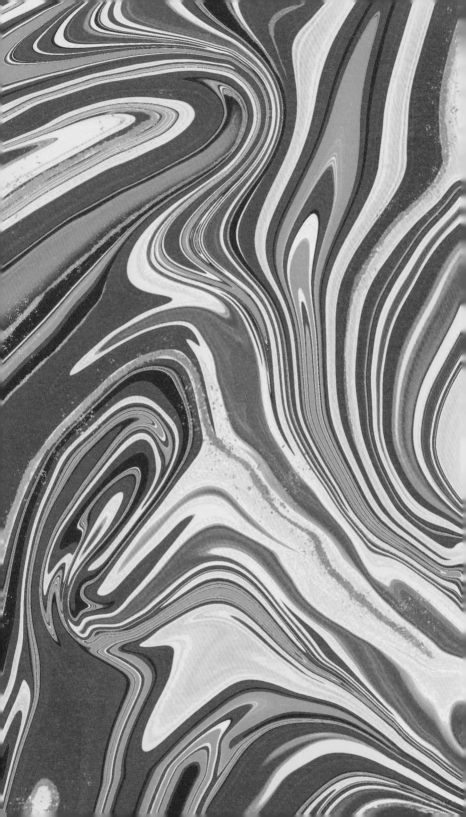